PUPPY LOVE

fLiRT

fLiRt

PUPPY LOVE

A. DESTINY AND CATHERINE HAPKA

SIMON PULSE

NEW YORK   LONDON   TORONTO   SYDNEY   NEW DELHI

SIMON PULSE

An imprint of Simon & Schuster Children's Publishing Division

1230 Avenue of the Americas, New York, NY 10020

First Simon Pulse edition September 2014

Text copyright © 2014 by Simon & Schuster, Inc.

Cover photograph copyright © 2014 by Plush Studios/Getty Images

All rights reserved, including the right of reproduction in whole or in part in any form.

SIMON PULSE and colophon are registered trademarks of Simon & Schuster, Inc.

For information about special discounts for bulk purchases, please contact Simon & Schuster Special Sales at 1-866-506-1949 or business@simonandschuster.com.

The Simon & Schuster Speakers Bureau can bring authors to your live event. For more information or to book an event contact the Simon & Schuster Speakers Bureau at 1-866-248-3049 or visit our website at www.simonspeakers.com.

Book design by Regina Flath

The text of this book was set in Adobe Caslon Pro.

Manufactured in the United States of America

10 9 8 7 6 5 4 3 2

Library of Congress Control Number 2013051005

ISBN 978-1-4424-8412-2 (pbk)

ISBN 978-1-4424-8414-6 (eBook)

PUPPY LOVE

Chapter ● One
Saturday morning

Would you hang on to that thing?" Robert complained as he steered into the turn lane for the Maple View Shopping Center. "Because if your crazy beast pees in my new car, I'm totally going Cruella De Vil on him."

"Muckle is not a *thing*." I grabbed my sheltie puppy in mid-leap. He was supposed to be sitting on my lap, but he'd spent most of the ten-minute drive clambering around trying to look out every window in the car at once. "And in case you haven't noticed," I added, "this car hasn't been new since the days of the horse and buggy."

Robert let out a snort and flipped back the lock of dark hair he'd been wearing gelled down over one eye lately. Retro goth? Who knew. Robert tended to create his own styles. "*So* not the point," he muttered.

I could tell by his wounded tone that my snarky comment had hit a sore spot. That was the thing about my best friend, the one and only Robert James Chase. I'd never have told him so, but he dished it out a lot better than he took it. He totally thought of himself as a superconfident future celebrity, tossing off witty one-liners and just generally being fabulous. In reality? He was a lot less ready for prime time than he thought he was. It was so easy to get under his skin it wasn't even funny. For instance, all you had to do was call him Robby or Bob instead of Robert, and he'd sulk for the rest of the day.

Anyway, he'd been expecting automotive luxury for his sixteenth birthday a couple of months earlier, which hadn't seemed like such a long shot. His parents had more money than they knew what to do with, and they drove top-of-the-line sports cars themselves. So imagine his surprise when the big day arrived and they presented him with a sturdy, practical Volvo station wagon older than he was.

As Robert pulled said Volvo land boat into the parking lot, Muckle was wiggling in my arms like only a three-and-a-half-month-old Shetland sheepdog puppy can wiggle. Or so I assumed. I'd only been a dog owner for a little over six weeks, so I was still getting the hang of it.

"Anyway, it's probably illegal to drive with him jumping around like that," Robert added sullenly. "I mean, they don't even let you text and drive, and having some weirdo puppy boinging off your face is way more distracting."

"Whatever." I was tired of his whining. After yanking a chunk of my wavy blah-brown hair out of Muckle's slobbery little mouth, I reached over and cranked up the music. My favorite CD was playing—the latest by the amazing Scottish band Skerrabra. Their lead singer, Corc, was just about the hottest guy I'd ever seen. Possibly the hottest guy who'd ever lived.

Hearing his incredible voice even made Robert look happier. His crush on Corc was only slightly less epic than mine.

"Herc we go—you've reached your destination, me bonny hen," Robert announced in a pretty fair imitation of Corc's sexy Scottish brogue. He pulled to the curb in front of the local PetzBiz superstore, leaving the Volvo idling loudly. "I'll be back to pick you up in an hour."

"Wait, what?" I blinked at him in surprise. "Aren't you coming in with us?"

Robert sighed, smoothing down the lapels of his vintage Hawaiian shirt. Did I mention that Robert has an interesting sense of style? "Things to do. Places to be. People to see. You know how it is."

"But—" I wasn't sure what to say. This was going to be a whole new thing for me, and I didn't do that well with new things. I wasn't shy, exactly. Just not quite the opposite of shy either. Being with Robert usually helped, though. He was so opposite of shy that it wasn't funny, and some of that usually rubbed off on me when we were together.

"Go get 'em, kid." Robert checked his watch. "You don't want to be late."

"But I thought you were coming too," I said. "You know—for moral support."

"What do you need me for? You're the dog girl." He grinned and winked. "Later, chica."

"Fine." I frowned at him. "You're right, we'll be great. Come on, Muckle—let's go."

Muckle barked and wiggled at the sound of his name. I clipped on his new leather leash and opened the door, bracing myself as he went flying out with his usual heedless enthusiasm. For a ten-pound puppy, he could exert a lot of force.

"Okay then." I hesitated another moment, wondering if Robert would change his mind. But he was humming along with Corc, not even looking at me. "See you in an hour."

I was tempted to fall on my knees right there on the curb and beg him to come in with me after all. There was nothing Robert loved more than a dramatic scene—it would probably work.

Then again, I could get back in the car and tell him to forget it. Suggest we go shopping or something instead, maybe hit the thrift shops in search of new looks for the Disguise Game . . . (More on that later.)

But no. When I looked at Muckle sniffing eagerly at the sidewalk, with his silky reddish-brown-and-white fur, his constantly wagging tail, and his adorably perky expression, I knew I couldn't blow this off. There was too much at stake.

Besides, I could do this. Even without Robert by my side, I could do it. I am Lauren, hear me roar.

"Okay, see you," I told Robert, slamming the car door with a little more force than absolutely necessary.

As the Volvo pulled away in a cloud of noxious exhaust, I squinted up at PetzBiz, which did its best to live up to its status as a big box store by being the biggest, boxiest store in the strip mall. Muckle zipped around me, trying to smell everything at once, then suddenly leaped into the air and started barking like a maniac. Another dog barked back, its yips almost as high-pitched and excited as the Muckster's. Which was really saying something, since my mother claimed Muckle's bark could shatter glass. And possibly human eardrums as well.

When I glanced over my shoulder, I saw another puppy around Muckle's size running toward us. He looked like some kind of terrier crossed with who-knew-what, with cute floppy ears, gangly legs that looked too long for his stout body, and an alert, foxy face.

On the other end of the leash, letting himself be dragged by the dog, was a guy around my age. I couldn't help noticing that he was even cuter than his puppy, even though he wasn't anywhere near my usual type. I tended to go for artsy, exotic guys—long hair, cool accents, brooding expressions. Well, at least in theory. I'd never actually had a boyfriend, so this was all mostly daydreams and unrequited crushes.

In any case, this guy wasn't like my imaginary boyfriends at all. He was more like an all-American jock, with broad shoulders, smooth dark skin without a zit to be seen, and a nice smile. He was even dressed in the typical jock uniform: jeans, sneakers, and a preppy rugby shirt.

"Hi," the guy said breathlessly as his dog dragged him up to me. Or more specifically, up to Muckle. "Are you here for the puppy kindergarten?"

"Yeah." I glanced down as the two pups started sniffing each other's rear ends. "You too?"

"Uh-huh." The guy grinned. "I probably should've signed up for the remedial class, though. Let's just say that obedience isn't Ozzy's strong point."

I smiled back. He really was awfully cute. And no, I wasn't looking at the dog. "Sounds like Muckle."

"Muckle?" The guy glanced at my sheltie. "Is that your puppy's name?"

"It's short for Muckle Roe. That's the name of one of the Shetland Islands in Scotland—they're these little islands up between the Atlantic and the North Sea." I didn't know why I was bothering with the lengthy explanations—most people sort of glazed over when I started geeking out about one of my little research projects. The thing was, this guy was even better-looking up close, and that always made me nervous. And being nervous made me babble. "He's a sheltie—you know, Shetland sheepdog. Like from the Shetland Islands, you know?" Duh, Lauren. "So I just figured his name should be—"

I never got to finish my explanation. At that moment Muckle decided the terrier mix looked threatening, or maybe he just got bored with the butt sniffing. In any case, he leaped at Ozzy with one of the wild, silly growls he made whenever he got worked up. The other puppy dodged just in time, bowing down on his front legs to invite Muckle to play. Muckle seemed to take that as an insult; he spun in a circle, barking loudly with his ears pinned back.

"Muckle, chill!" I cried, barely hanging on to the leash as he lunged toward the other puppy again. I leaned forward to grab him, but just then Ozzy seemed to realize that Muckle looked kind of scary. He zigged just as I zagged, and my foot caught on his leash. Suddenly I felt myself going airborne.

"Yaargh!" I yelled.

"Careful!" Ozzy's owner exclaimed.

He jumped forward, placing himself between me and the sidewalk. I let out a very ladylike "Oof!" as I plowed into him. He grabbed me by the upper arms and hauled me back onto my feet.

"You okay?" he asked.

I was very aware of his hands—his big, strong hands—still encircling my arms. My eyes were inches from his biceps, which I couldn't help noticing were nicely flexed as he steadied me. For a second I was extremely distracted by the nice smell coming from him—a clean smell, like soap and shampoo and laundry detergent, with maybe the slightest hint of eau de wet dog. . . .

"Are you okay?" he asked again.

I blinked, coming back to my senses. Sort of.

"Um, yeah." I carefully took half a step back. He let go of my arms and stepped back as well.

Miraculously, I still had Muckle's leash clutched tightly in my hand. Muckle chose that moment to leap away in pursuit of a leaf blowing past. I staggered slightly, but managed to stay on my own two feet this time.

The cute guy was still staring at me. His dog was sitting behind him, peering around his owner's legs at Muckle.

"I'm fine," I said a little too loudly. "Thanks. Um, I'd better get inside."

Spinning around, I hurried into the store, wondering exactly what was wrong with me. I also realized it was a good thing Robert wasn't there. He would have been rolling on the sidewalk laughing at my dorkiness. I could hear his voice in my head: *Smooth move, Lauren. But you're supposed to make the guys fall all over themselves for you, not the other way around. . . .*

Yeah. Imaginary Robert was so right. This was exactly why I'd never had a real boyfriend. I was mostly fine talking to people—teachers, other girls, Robert, non-cute guys, adults, little kids, miscellaneous random strangers. But put a cute guy in front of me and I turned into a blithering idiot.

I'd pretty much proved that a few too many times at parties and school dances and other places where cute guys tended to congregate. By this time I'd pretty much given up, decided to stick to my daydreams about Corc and forget trying to interact with real, live guys.

Pathetic? Yes. But it seemed safer that way. It just wasn't worth the humiliation to keep trying. This latest encounter only proved it.

Chapter ● Two
A few minutes later

I'd become very familiar with the PetzBiz superstore since becoming a dog owner six weeks earlier. Dragging Muckle away from a tempting display of rawhide chews set conveniently at puppy eye level, I headed for the training area at the back. It basically consisted of the "training ring," which was an open area with mats on the floor and a waist-high movable plastic wall to keep the dogs more or less contained.

As usual for a Saturday, the store was packed. People and dogs were everywhere, and within a few steps Muckle was bouncing around like a jumping bean. I could see the signs that his tiny brain was becoming overwhelmed with all the new sights, sounds, and smells, so I quickly scooped him up and tucked him under my arm. I'd nearly fallen on my face once already this morning because of him, and I wasn't in the mood for a rerun.

When I arrived at the training ring, there was only one puppy inside its plastic walls, a floppy-eared hound. I recognized the pup's owner—she was a serious-looking girl a year or two older than me who waitressed on the weekends at my parents' favorite Italian bistro. I waved at her, but she didn't see me. She was staring intently at her puppy, telling it repeatedly to sit as it continued to wander around, smelling everything within range. With a shrug, I turned away and set Muckle down near the entrance.

"Behave," I told him strictly. "You don't want to get kicked out of class before it even starts, right? I mean, if you can't hack it in puppy kindergarten, you'll never get into puppy college."

"So this is the training area, right?"

It was Ozzy's owner. Okay, so maybe I shouldn't have been surprised that he'd followed me to the training ring. I already knew he was there for the puppy training class. And he didn't look like the type of guy to get scared off too easily. Not even by having some psycho girl and her even more psycho dog make fools of themselves in front of him.

No, that wasn't the surprising part. The surprising part? He was smiling at me. Seeming to still want to talk to me. Me, as in Psycho Girl.

"Um, yeah," I blurted out. "I, uh, checked it out when I was here buying Muckle's food the other day."

As witty banter went, it wasn't exactly genius level. But the guy chuckled.

"I'm Jamal, by the way," he said. "Jamal Hughes. And this is Ozzy."

I noticed he was keeping his puppy on a pretty short leash. Probably afraid that Cujo—also known as Muckle—was going to launch another attack. Fortunately, Muckle seemed to have gotten over it. He was sitting beside me, sniffing curiously in the direction of the other puppy.

"I'm Lauren Parker," I said. "And you already met Muckle."

Muckle cocked his head and stared up at me when he heard his name. His ears pricked in my direction, and he looked so adorable that I had to smile.

"He's adorable," Jamal commented. "So, I've never seen you at school, Lauren. Do you go to MVHS?"

His gaze slid quickly up and down me in that certain way guys have when they're trying to check a girl out without letting her know he's doing it. Yeah, that's right. Jamal was checking me out. I couldn't help feeling flattered. Most of the guys at school barely acknowledged my existence, let alone looked at me like I was, well, a girl. Obviously the guys at MVHS—that was Maple View High, the local public school—were a little less choosy.

"I go to County Day Academy," I told Jamal, trying not to worry about whether my cheeks were going pink again. "I'm a sophomore."

"Oh! Private school girl, huh? Duh, I should've known."

I tensed. "What do you mean?"

He flashed me that friendly smile again. "Just saying, I'm sure

I would have noticed you if you went to my school. I'm a sophomore too, by the way."

I relaxed. Some people in my town had kind of an attitude about County Day Academy. It was one of the most selective private high schools in the state, and it wasn't exactly cheap, either. My parents loved to talk about the advantages my County Day education was supposed to be giving me, even though my mom had to cut way back on her monthly shopping-and-hairdressing expenditures when I started there.

"Look, I think Ozzy and Muckle are making friends." Jamal nodded toward the puppies. They were doing that butt-sniffing thing again, but this time both their tails were wagging happily—Ozzy's stubby little wire-haired one and Muck's long, fluffy one.

"Sorry about before." I kept a careful eye on Muckle, not wanting a repeat of what had happened outside. "He's usually friendly with other dogs, but he's kind of easily overstimulated."

"That's cool." Jamal bent down and ruffled Muckle's ears. "He's a cute little guy. How'd you end up with him? Is he purebred?"

"Yeah. I found the breeder online—she lives about an hour from here." I stepped aside as a pair of giggling girls hurried into the training ring. They both looked about thirteen years old. One was carrying a tiny Chihuahua puppy, while the other was trying to hang on to the leash attached to an exuberant retriever pup.

"Looks like the rest of the class is starting to get here," Jamal said.

"Yeah." I heard the scrabbling of dog claws against the linoleum floor and glanced behind me. A cool-looking puppy with long legs and a sleek orangey-colored coat was rushing toward us, dragging a pretty girl around our age at the other end of its leash. The girl had straight ash-blond hair and a sweet, heart-shaped face that would have fit right in in some Victorian costume drama.

"Whoa!" With a laugh, Jamal stepped in and grabbed the orange pup, swooping it up into his arms even though it had to weigh at least twenty-five pounds. "Hey, Gizi girl. What's up, Rachel?"

"Thanks for stopping her," Rachel said breathlessly, smiling at Jamal as he set her puppy down. Then she noticed me standing there and ducked her head shyly. "Sorry—I hope my dog didn't scare yours."

"No worries." I glanced at Muckle, who was staring up at the taller orange puppy with pricked ears. "I've never seen a dog like that before. What is it?"

"Gizi's a vizsla." Rachel tucked a strand of hair behind her ear. "That's like a Hungarian hunting dog."

I found myself staring at Rachel. I'd always wanted my hair to do that thing hers did—lie flat and sleek and elegant, like the vizsla's coat. Instead my semi-wavy, semi-frizzy brown hair was doomed to usually looking almost as fluffy as my own pup's fur. And that look worked a lot better on Muckle than it did on me.

I lifted my free hand, trying to quickly pat my hair down. "Uh, I'm Lauren. Are you in this class too?"

Rachel nodded. "We're taking it for the second time."

"She's the one who told me about it," Jamal put in. "I overheard her talking about it in English class. She was telling her friends how Gizi flunked out last time. Isn't that right, girl?" He laughed and gave the vizsla puppy a pat. Gizi's entire body wiggled in response, and she leaped up at him with a joyful bark.

Muckle and Ozzy both barked too. Gizi turned, still wiggling all over, and leaped toward them with the exuberance only a hyper puppy can show. Ozzy started doing the play bowing thing, but Muckle jumped straight up in the air.

"Muckle, no!" I cried as I felt the leash slip out of my hand.

Muckle let out an excited bark as he realized he was free! Free! Free! He jumped right over Ozzy, who was still bowing hopefully in Gizi's direction, and took off toward the middle of the store.

"Sorry!" Rachel exclaimed, dragging her puppy back with a hand on her collar. But it was too late; Muckle was already ten yards away and still going, dragging his leash behind him. His legs might have looked short, but they could move fast.

I was already running after him, following the sound of his high-pitched barks. "Muckle, get back here!" I hollered. "Come, boy! Come!"

He disappeared down one of the aisles. Skidding around the corner, I saw that the shelves were packed with canned cat food. Muckle barely paused to sniff at them before racing on around the next corner.

"Oh, you rotten thing," I muttered. "Muckle! Come back here!"

The barking stopped suddenly. Uh-oh. Various possibilities

flashed through my mind. Option one, Muckle had found a puppy-height display of edibles and was now stuffing his greedy little face with the eleventy-twelve pounds of liver snaps or pig's ears or gerbil food I'd have to beg Robert for the money to pay for. Option two, he'd become a snack himself for a cranky Rottweiler or something. Option three, he'd gone into stealth mode on purpose just to drive me crazy.

Yes, I knew dogs didn't really think like that. Sometimes, though? I had to wonder. Especially when Muckle peed on Mom's favorite Persian rug for the third day in a row, as he'd done just the day before. Which was part of the reason we were here, come to think of it. . . .

All of this went tumbling through my mind as I sprinted around the corner. I was moving so fast that it took an extra second or two to register the guy standing in front of me, cradling my dog in his arms.

I skidded to a stop just in time to avoid crashing into them. The guy was rubbing Muckle's fuzzy head, and Muckle was gazing up at him adoringly.

Not that I blamed him. The guy was a little older than me, maybe seventeen or so. More importantly, he was the most gorgeous guy I'd ever seen in real life. Like, almost on the Corc scale. He was tall and lean, with dark hair, pale skin, and ice-blue eyes.

"Oh, hello," he said, glancing up and locking his gaze on mine. "Is this your runaway puppy?"

My jaw dropped. I couldn't believe my ears—he had an accent!

"Are you Scottish?" I blurted out.

One corner of his mouth twitched up. "Irish, actually," he said. "My family moved over from County Kildare when I was in middle school. But you were close."

"Oh. Sorry." My face flamed. *I know the difference between a Scottish and an Irish accent!* I wanted to scream. *I swear I totally do! I can even identify whether a speaker comes from north or south of the Firth of Tay, for Pete's sake!*

Yeah, no. Probably not the best way to impress him at that point. Instead, I smiled weakly and glanced at Muckle. He was cradled in Mr. Irish-Not-Scottish-Accent's arms, tongue flopping out and a look of bliss on his little puppy face. Clearly a dog with taste.

"Thanks for catching him," I said. "He pulled away and took off before I could catch him. He's not very good with obedience."

"It's okay, shelties can be tough at first. But they're very smart and trainable once you get their attention." He gave Muckle one last cuddle, then held him toward me.

As I took my puppy, my hand brushed against the guy's, and an electric jolt went through me from head to toe. For a second I felt dizzy, as if my fantasy life was colliding with the real one—as if Corc himself had just stepped into my local suburban strip mall and was about to whisk me away to enjoy the life of romance and adventure I'd always dreamed of. . . .

"So you should bring him to my puppy K," the guy said. "I've got a class for teen handlers starting right now, actually."

I blinked at the vision of male perfection before me. "Wait— you're teaching the puppy class?" I exclaimed. "We're in that class!"

If he noticed how over-the-top geeky-psyched I sounded, he didn't let on. "Cool," he said with a smile. "I'm Adam O'Connell, by the way. Certified dog trainer."

"Lauren," I said, pointing to myself. "Certified spazzy-puppy owner. And this is Muckle. Certifiable."

Adam laughed as if my joke had actually been funny. "Charmed." His smile lit up the store, putting the overhead fluorescents to shame. "Come along then, Lauren and Muckle. Let's get over there and get started, what do you say?"

"Sure." I smiled up at him, still dazzled. Suddenly the difficulties of the past six weeks melted away. It had all been worth it, because it had led to this. Fate. Kismet. Destiny. Basically, a dream come true. Even though at the time it had seemed to be turning into a nightmare. . . .

Chapter ● Three
Six weeks earlier

You don't have to do this, you know."

I looked up from consulting the Google Maps directions I'd printed out the night before. "What's with you, anyway?" I asked Robert. "You've been saying that since we left my driveway an hour ago."

He shrugged, not looking at me. "I'm just saying. A dog is a huge pain in the patootie."

Robert was probably the only sixteen-year-old in existence who'd use the word "patootie." If it was even a real word, which I doubted.

"Turn left up by that church," I told him. "We should be almost there."

A shiver ran through me as I said it. Almost there. Almost to the breeder's house, where my lifelong dreams would finally come true. I was picking up my puppy today. My. Puppy. I could hardly believe it.

I'd wanted a dog my whole life, pretty much. At least since the day when I was five years old and went to a friend's house to play, and fell in love with their sweet older Lab. After that, I'd dreamed of becoming a dog owner myself.

The reason it hadn't happened for another ten years? My older sister, Britt. She was deathly allergic. Which meant no pets for me—until now. Britt had left for the University of Virginia two weeks earlier, and my parents had finally agreed to let me get a puppy. Of course, I had to promise to pay for the pup and all its expenses myself, and to do all the work involved. Oh, and to make sure whichever canine I got didn't wreck the house, which was their pride and joy. Especially Mom's. She loved redecorating the place almost as much as she loved redecorating herself at Neiman Marcus and the local spa.

"Seriously, though," Robert said. "It's not too late to back out. I have my phone—we can call this breeder chick, say we had a flat tire or something. . . ."

"Give it a rest, okay?" I scowled at him. "It would be nice if you could be at least a little supportive. This is only the most exciting thing I've ever done."

"Bringing home some bag of fur? If you say so." He eyed me. "Anyway, I am being supportive. I'm driving you to pick the mutt up, aren't I?"

"That doesn't count. You'd drive anyone anywhere." That was true, and he knew it. He'd earned his license less than a month earlier, and the novelty hadn't worn off yet. Slumping down in my seat, I consulted the directions again, then glanced out the window. We'd just left another tiny town behind, and thick forest lined both sides of the quiet country highway. "Wow, this place is really out in the middle of nowhere," I said, hoping we weren't going the wrong way.

"Yeah." He flicked his gaze toward me. "Don't a whole bunch of those stupid horror flicks you love so much start exactly like this?"

I chose to ignore that. Robert had never appreciated my taste in films. "Tell me again why you didn't want to borrow your dad's GPS?" I asked instead.

"I don't believe in going where some high-tech gizmo tells me to go," Robert informed me with a flicker of his usual spirit. "I believe in charting my own path, creating my own trail, following my own—"

"Turn there!" I interrupted, waving the paper at him. "Quick! Right there!"

Robert spun the wheel, squealing around the corner onto a tiny side road. The car thumped over a rut with a moan of protest from the springs.

"Are you sure this is right?" Robert asked, slowing down a little. He glanced dubiously at the tiny houses that appeared wherever the woods thinned out a bit. Most of them looked kind of worn out, with ragged lawns and sagging shutters.

"I think so." I checked the printout again. "Yeah, this has got to be it. How many Raccoon Roads can there be around here? Now watch for number seventeen."

Number seventeen turned out to be a brick ranch with a chain-link fence around its small, mostly dirt yard. A dog raced out of the house and barked at us as Robert pulled carefully into the narrow gravel driveway.

I smiled with relief. "Look, a sheltie—this is it!"

Robert cut the engine and glanced around. "Doesn't look quite like it did on the website, does it?"

He was right, but I didn't bother to respond. The sheltie was gorgeous, with a thick sable coat and an alert expression. I wondered if it was my puppy's father.

"Come on, let's go—we're late," I said, unclipping my seat belt.

By the time we climbed out of the car, a woman had come out onto the front stoop and called the sheltie over to her. She was in her forties or so, with a tired, pasty face and a knot of thinning light-brown hair twisted on top of her head. Her hands and feet were petite, but the rest of her was . . . not.

"Hi!" I called to her. "I'm Lauren. Is Vicky here?"

"I'm Vicky." The woman gave me a weary smile. "Come on in, honey."

"Oh. Um, thanks." I tried to hide my surprise. Vicky wasn't what I'd been expecting either. There had been no pictures of her on the website or anything, but there'd been lots of text talking about all the fun stuff she did with her dogs, from agility and obedience competitions to long walks in the woods. I'd formed a picture in my head of someone youthful and active and cool. Someone a little younger and, well, more athletic-looking.

But never mind. You weren't supposed to judge a book by its cover, right?

"This is my friend Robert," I told Vicky, gesturing for Robert to come join me. "He came along to help."

Vicky glanced at Robert and did a double take. No wonder. We weren't supposed to be playing the Disguise Game today, but that didn't mean he looked normal. He was dressed in his favorite vintage pink bowling shirt with one of his dad's prep school ties knotted over it.

"Come on in, kids," Vicky said. "Your puppy's waiting for you." She turned and heaved herself back up the step, disappearing into the house. The sheltie went with her.

I traded a look with Robert. He actually looked more alert and interested than he'd been all day. Unlike me, he enjoys it when things don't go as expected. I rolled my eyes at him, then followed Vicky inside.

Her house smelled like dog poo and burned milk. A loud chorus of barking erupted as soon as we entered, and half a dozen more shelties came pouring into the tiny, dimly lit front room from every direction. Soon we were surrounded.

"Boys! Girls! Down, please," Vicky ordered. "We have guests."

Most of the dogs obeyed, though one cute little blue merle

insisted on continuing to sniff Robert's crotch. Robert eyed the sheltie with suspicion.

"The puppies are back here," Vicky said, heading through a doorway that turned out to lead into the kitchen.

The place was small and even smellier than the rest of the house. A round wooden table and several chairs had been pushed back to make room for a large exercise pen. Newspaper covered most of the linoleum, and the sink was full of unwashed dishes.

But I hardly noticed any of that. My gaze went straight to the half-dozen adorable sheltie puppies running around the pen. As we approached, one of the adult dogs separated itself from the rest of the pack and jumped the low barrier into the x-pen.

"That's Bella, the mother," Vicky said. "Your puppy is the little sable in the corner there."

"Wait, doesn't she get to pick out her own dog?" Robert put in.

"That's not how it works." I shot him a glare, wishing he'd listened better when I'd explained all this. "Vicky chooses a puppy for me based on what I told her I'm looking for. After all, she knows the pups best."

"Yeah. Like I said, yours is this one right here." Vicky leaned over and scooped up one of the adorable bundles of fur. "Male, like you wanted."

"Oh, he's beautiful!" I cradled the pup gingerly, though I tightened my grip slightly when he wiggled so vigorously that he almost sprung right out of my hands.

I'd read online that dog breeders usually asked potential buyers lots of questions about themselves, to make sure they could provide the right kind of home for their precious puppies. In our online exchanges, Vicky had mostly just inquired what color puppy I preferred and whether I wanted a male or a female. But I figured she'd probably been waiting to size me up in person before getting to the interview stuff. I'd always been a little bit of an overachiever, so I was ready to volunteer the information before she had to ask.

"So like I told you, this will be my first dog," I said, cuddling my puppy—my puppy!—against my chest. "But I've always adored dogs, and I've read a ton to prepare myself . . ." I babbled on for a while, telling her about Britt's allergies and my deal with my parents, the vet I'd picked out, and the food I planned to feed.

"Good, good," Vicky said when I paused for breath.

"Oh, and in case you're wondering why I decided to get a sheltie," I went on, "it's mostly because my grandparents live on a farm in Vermont, and they have a collie. She's an amazing dog—I always spend tons of time with her when we visit, and I love her. So I'm definitely partial to herding breeds. And I figured a sheltie was the perfect size for a suburban house, so that's why I chose the breed."

Out of the corner of my eye, I could see Robert smirking. He knew the real reason I'd settled on a sheltie. In a word: Corc. My crush on him had expanded into an obsession with all things Scottish.

Still, my grandparents' collie truly was an awesome dog. That had helped make up my mind too. At least a little.

"Anyway," I said quickly, not wanting to give Robert a chance to throw in any "witty" comments, "I'm also hoping to maybe get into some dog sports eventually. You said the parents have both competed in stuff, right?"

"Uh-huh." Vicky leaned over again, sliding a piece of newspaper over a wet spot on the linoleum. "My dogs do a little of everything."

I barely heard her. The puppy in my arms had managed to wiggle himself into a position where he could reach up and lick my chin. As I felt his warm pink tongue on my skin and breathed in his puppy scent, my heart melted and all rational thought dissolved from my brain. If Vicky had more questions for me, she was going to have to ask them and hope I wasn't too addlepated to answer.

"Aren't you the cutest thing ever?" I cooed at the puppy, who let out a happy yip and wagged his entire body.

"So how did you want to pay?" Vicky asked, breaking into the lovefest.

I looked up at her. "I brought cash," I said. Giving the puppy one last squeeze and setting him back in the x-pen, I dug into my pocket for the wad of bills I'd stuffed in there. "Is that all right?"

"Of course." Vicky stepped over to a tall stack of paperwork balanced on top of the microwave. "Let me just find a copy of the contract."

"She has to sign a contract?" Robert said.

"Yes. I told you about that, remember?" I glared at him. Now that I was madly in love with my puppy, I definitely didn't want him to mess things up.

Vicky pulled a sheaf of papers out of the stack. "Here it is," she said. Then she glanced at Robert. "By the way, one of my buyers backed out, so I have an extra puppy available," she told him. "Male, sweet, very healthy. You interested?"

"Me?" Robert looked as shocked as if she'd just suggested he take up cannibalism or something. "Um, no. Thanks."

Vicky shrugged. "You sure? All right, just figured I'd ask." She handed me the contract, then scrabbled around in a drawer until she found a pen.

While I signed the contract, Vicky bustled around the tiny kitchen, tossing things into a big paper shopping bag. "The puppy comes with a week's supply of food," she said. "You'll want to make any diet changes slowly. You also get a free toy and a booklet about shelties."

"Great." My puppy was wrestling with one of his siblings. I smiled as I watched his tiny, fluffy tail wag and listened to his playful little growls and yaps. I didn't want to interrupt the puppies' game, but Vicky seemed to have no such concern. Reaching down, she grabbed my puppy, gave him a kiss on the top of the head, and handed him to me.

"Here you go," she said. "Feel free to e-mail me with any questions. But I'm sure you'll do great."

"Oh. Um, thanks." Was it my imagination, or was she pretty much telling us to get out? I'd been hoping to talk to her more about how to get involved in dog sports, maybe ask for a demo from some of her adult shelties. . . .

But never mind. As my puppy settled himself against my chest, a warm glow filled me. I had a dog. A special, lively little sheltie pup, all my own. Finally my dreams had come true.

"Ready, chica?" Robert sounded impatient. "We should probably hit the road. It's a long drive home."

"Okay, okay, we're coming." I smiled down at my puppy. "Isn't that right, little guy? It's time for you to come home."

Chapter ● Four
Meanwhile, back at puppy K . . .

I followed Adam—lovely, gorgeous Adam—back to the training ring. By the time we got there, more people had arrived with their puppies. Jamal and Rachel were still hovering near the entrance.

"Oh, good, you caught him!" Rachel sounded relieved. "Sorry again about that."

"It's okay. Actually, Adam caught him." I glanced over at Adam with what I hoped was an appealing smile, one that made me look cool and smart and confident and much less inept than all evidence indicated.

But he wasn't paying attention to me anymore. He checked his watch, then walked into the ring.

"Hello, everyone!" He clapped his hands, which made several of the puppies, including Muckle, start barking. "Whoever's here for the puppy kindergarten class for teens, come on in and let's get started, all right?"

"That guy's our teacher?" Jamal sounded surprised. "I think he was in my study hall last year."

"Yeah. His name's Adam—he's a senior," Rachel told him. "He's amazing with dogs. He's the one who told me not to give up on Gizi—said vizslas take a while to settle down, but when they do, they're great dogs."

"So Adam goes to your school? That's cool." I tried not to sound totally envious. What would it be like to walk the halls between classes and see that passing by?

Then again, maybe it was better that I didn't have to deal with all that magnificence in an academic setting. Too distracting.

Inside the ring, the other members of the class—the human ones, that is—were taking seats on the folding chairs set up along the perimeter of the training ring. In addition to the Chihuahua, retriever, and hound I'd seen earlier, there were now a roly-poly pug puppy and a middle-size brown-and-white mixed breed that looked like every dog in the AKC catalog all rolled into one.

"There's three seats together over there," Jamal said. "Let's grab them."

Rachel and I followed him. I was still holding Muckle, and Rachel was keeping Gizi tightly at her side on a short leash. But Jamal wasn't paying much attention to Ozzy, and as he headed for the empty chairs, the terrier cross-bounded forward and knocked over a bucket sitting in the middle of the ring. About a pound of liver treats tumbled out.

"Oops, sorry!" Jamal grabbed his puppy, trying to pry open Ozzy's jaws to remove the three or four liver treats he'd snapped up.

"It's all right, mate, let him have it." Adam wandered over and started picking up the treats. "Take a seat, all right?"

"Sure. Sorry." Jamal dragged Ozzy away, looking sheepish. "Well, that's a good way for Oz to impress his teacher on the first day, huh?" he muttered to me and Rachel when he joined us.

Rachel giggled. "Don't worry. Adam won't hold it against him," she said. "Against you, maybe. But not against the dog."

Jamal grinned and dropped into the chair beside mine. Rachel sat down on my other side. I set Muckle on the ground, though I made sure to keep a firm hold on his leash. I might have gotten off on the wrong foot in terms of impressing Adam with my puppy-handling skills, but I was determined to do much better from now on. Maybe he'd be so awestruck that he'd insist on becoming my boyfriend immediately.

The thought made me blush. It also made me miss what Adam said next. I snapped back to reality when I realized everyone else was standing up.

"Huh?" I said, turning to Rachel. "Um, sorry. What'd he say?"

"He wants us to lead our puppies around in a big circle," Rachel whispered. "That way he can see where we are in our leash training."

"Oh." I gulped. So far, Muckle's "leash training" consisted of me trying to keep up as he dragged me along the sidewalks and through people's yards in our subdivision. "Okay. Come on, Muck. Heel or whatever."

Muckle spun in a circle as all the other puppies started to move. He let out a few ear-piercing barks, then leaped happily at Gizi.

"No, Muckle. Down!" I cried.

Adam heard me and hurried over. "It's all right, no need to get angry," he told me. "He doesn't know any better yet. That's why you're here, eh?"

"Yeah." I smiled at him, a little blinded by his beauty. He smiled back briefly before hurrying over to help the girl with the pug, which didn't seem to be in the mood for walking, since it kept flopping over and rolling around on its back.

From that point on, Muckle made impressing the teacher extremely difficult. He jumped around, he barked at shoppers passing by outside the training ring, he tried to harass the other dogs. Generally, he behaved—or, rather, misbehaved—like his usual unruly self.

My only comfort was that Jamal and Rachel were also having trouble. Gizi wouldn't sit still for more than a microsecond, while Ozzy was alternately boisterous, clueless, and stubborn.

"He's usually not quite this bad, I swear," Jamal murmured to me after dragging Ozzy back to our seats. The two of them had just totally flunked their loose-leash walking lesson.

"It's okay," I whispered back, keeping one eye on Adam, who

was helping the Chihuahua attempt the exercise. Okay, maybe more than one eye. "Adam seems to think Ozzy's doing fine."

"Yeah, maybe you're right." Jamal smiled at me. Even with at least one eye on Adam, I couldn't help noticing Jamal was giving me that look again. That I'm-noticing-you're-a-girl look.

But I tried to just take it as a compliment and forget it. After all, I had no need to flirt with him or anyone else. I'd already met the perfect man.

"Lauren? You coming?"

I realized the perfect man was talking to me. And staring at me as if he thought I might be a little slow. My face went hot as I realized that while I'd been staring at him, possibly with drool involved, he'd been calling me and Muckle up for our turn. Oops.

"We're coming," I blurted out. I jumped up so quickly that I surprised Muckle, who was actually taking a rest break under my seat. He let out a yelp as I yanked him bodily forward.

"Easy with the leash," Adam said. "Give him a chance to figure out what you're doing and choose to come along, rather than forcing him."

Oops again. "Sorry," I said to both Adam and Muckle. "Now what do you want us to do?"

Muckle turned out to be a bit better at loose-leash walking than Ozzy, but not by much. Still, I hoped Adam noticed the way I was paying attention and trying to do exactly as he instructed. That had always won me points with my teachers at school. Maybe it would work in this case too.

The last ten minutes of class involved Adam supervising our puppies while they were allowed to play freely with one another. At last—something Muckle was good at. He ran around, jumping on the other puppies and having a total blast. Adam had to stop him from squashing the Chihuahua once or twice, but otherwise everything went pretty well.

"Okay, people," Adam said at last. "That's our time. See you all on Tuesday afternoon. In the meantime, keep working on the exercises we learned today, okay? Good class, all."

The girl with the retriever puppy giggled and clapped, and we all joined in. Adam grinned and swept into a bow. I was pretty sure he was just being funny, but he looked quite dashing regardless.

I grabbed Muckle and gave him a hug. "Good boy," I whispered into his silky fur. Over the top of his head, I glanced at Adam. He'd stopped near the edge of the ring and was chatting with the pug's owner. I really wanted to go over there and join them, get to know Adam better. Maybe even figure out if he'd felt that electric tingle when we touched earlier too.

But no. That wasn't going to happen. Me, Lauren the wimp, go up to a hot guy and start chatting him up? Yeah, that was about as likely as Muckle winning first prize in an obedience competition.

"So that was fun, huh?" Jamal's voice broke into my thoughts. He'd snapped Ozzy's leash back on.

"Yeah." I set Muckle down and leashed him as well. Rachel joined us, and the three of us walked out of the store together, discussing the class. I held my breath as we passed Adam, hoping he'd say something to us. Well, to me. But he just smiled briefly and then returned to his conversation with the pug girl.

Oh well. I had seven and a half more weeks, Tuesdays and Saturdays, to convince him we were meant to be together. I was just going to have to figure out how to make the most of it. Maybe Robert could help—he was much more of a romantic than I was.

As we stepped outside, I glanced around for the big, boxy Volvo, but it was nowhere in sight. I hoped Robert hadn't forgotten he was supposed to pick me up. Sometimes when he got involved in shopping, he could forget the rest of the world existed.

"How are you two getting home?" Jamal asked. "My car's here if you need a ride."

"Thanks," Rachel said. "But my dad's picking me up."

"Me too," I said. Then I laughed. "I mean, Rachel's dad isn't picking me up, but I do have a ride coming."

"Oh. Cool." Jamal actually looked disappointed. He glanced down at Ozzy, who was sitting quietly at his feet. "Anyway, thanks for telling me about this class, Rachel. Look—it's working already! This is the least hyper Ozzy has been since I got him."

Rachel and I both laughed. "Muckle too," I agreed. My puppy wasn't being quite as quiet as Ozzy, but he was sniffing around with much less than his usual exuberance. His tail was wagging gently, and he seemed pretty mellow.

"I just hope Gizi does better this time," Rachel said, rubbing her puppy's head as the vizsla stared intently at a scrap of paper blowing past in the parking lot. "She's way more active than I was expecting when we got her."

"Tell me about it." Jamal rolled his eyes. "Ozzy seemed so nice and sane when I first saw him. He totally had me fooled!"

Rachel and I laughed again. I already felt pretty comfortable with both of them, which was kind of amazing. Like I said, I wasn't exactly shy. But I wasn't the type to bond instantly with total strangers, either.

"Where'd you get him?" I asked Jamal.

"The shelter over in Riverside," he replied. "I wanted a dog to run with."

"You run?" I said, mostly because it seemed like the polite thing to say. I had about as much interest in running as Muckle did in calculus. Or as I did in calculus, for that matter.

"I'm on the cross-country team at school, so I run almost every day," he replied. "I figured it'd be more fun with a dog along, you know?"

So he was a jock. Score one for judging a book by its cover.

"You should have told me," Rachel told Jamal with a smile. "You could've borrowed Gizi. She loves to run."

"By the way," I said to her, "I've been meaning to ask—how'd you come up with Gizi's name? It's really pretty."

"It's the name of some old Hungarian actress." Rachel shrugged. "My dad came up with it. He's super into anything Hungarian—his parents were both born over there, but they moved here years before he came along."

"That's cool." Jamal looked interested. "I never knew that. Did Lauren tell you she named Muckle after an island?"

"Yeah, Muckle Roe. It's Scottish, since he's a sheltie," I told the other girl.

Just then a large, spotlessly clean black sedan pulled up to the curb. The windows were rolled down, and a stern-looking man with a mustache leaned out the driver's side.

"Hello, Rachel," he called in a booming voice—the type of voice that demanded attention. "How did it go today?"

"Fine." Rachel gave a tug on Gizi's leash. "That's my dad. See you next time."

Jamal and I said good-bye, and both Muckle and Ozzy started jumping around again, trying to get at the car. Rachel patted both puppies, smiled shyly at us humans, then hurried over and got into the sedan with Gizi. Her father drove off immediately.

"Wow," I said. "Rachel's dad isn't what I was expecting after meeting her. She's so nice and sweet, but he seems a little scary. Is he always like that?"

"I don't know." Jamal shrugged. "I only have a couple of classes with her. And she seems pretty quiet."

"Oh." I realized Jamal and I were alone together. And he was giving me that look again. That look I wished I could get from Adam.

"So what's your story, Lauren?" Jamal said. "What do you like to do for fun? You know—besides try to keep up with your hyper puppy." He grinned and leaned down to give Muckle a pat.

"Oh, just the usual, I guess." I scanned the parking lot, hoping Robert would show up soon. "Hanging out, listening to music, you know."

He untangled the leash from around Ozzy's front leg. "What kind of music do you like?"

"All different stuff—alternative, postpunk, that kind of deal. My favorite band is Skerrabra."

"Ska-what?"

"Skerrabra," I echoed. "They're, um, Scottish."

"Just like Muckle! Cool." Jamal shrugged. "I don't think I know them, though. I mostly listen to rock and hip-hop. But if this Skaberra—"

"Skerrabra," I corrected.

"Yeah, them." He smiled at me. "Maybe I can borrow some of their stuff from you sometime—I'm always looking for music to work out to."

"Sure," I said politely, though I was pretty sure there wasn't much point in following through. Jamal didn't come across as the typical Skerrabra fan, to say the least.

Still, he was pretty cool for a jock. Even if he didn't know anything about music. Maybe it would be worth burning a CD for him. I could help him open up his mind to a whole new world of cool music. Wasn't that the sort of thing friends did for each other? And strangely, he was already feeling kind of like a friend. Even if we didn't have anything in common other than out-of-control puppies.

"Cool. Thanks." Jamal shifted his weight from one foot to the other and shot me a sidelong look. "Um, so Lauren—do you have a boyfriend?"

I froze, not sure what to say. What could I say? *I'm working on it?*

At that moment, in a roar of exhaust, the Volvo finally arrived. Robert squealed to a stop at the curb right in front of us, then leaped out with a flourish.

"Sorry I'm late, gorgeous!" he called out.

When I'd seen him last, he'd been dressed relatively normally in jeans and a Skerrabra concert tee. Now? He was decked out in a tuxedo and wingtips. Very James Bond.

Obviously he'd scored big at one of the local consignment shops and was ready for another installment of our favorite activity, the Disguise Game. That was our thing. We would dress up as different crazy characters, from sixties hippies to medical students to motorcycle gangsters, then go out and see who noticed and what happened. Robert had come up with the idea soon after we became friends. We'd been browsing in a thrift store and found matching neon pants straight out of the eighties. I'd taken a little convincing the first time or two—I wasn't as brave or attention-seeking as he was, to put it mildly. But then he'd asked me: *What's the worst that can happen?*

And just like that, I was convinced. Because he was right. What was the worst that could happen? I'd be embarrassed, and maybe the cool kids at County Day would make fun of me. Big whoop. Most of them were jerks anyway. Why live my life for them?

And you know what? It had turned out to be fun. It felt strangely exhilarating to walk around disguised as someone else, a different kind of person, one who didn't care what anyone thought. One who lived a whole different kind of life from the real me. The boring, everyday, nondisguised me.

Jamal seemed startled by Robert's sudden arrival. "Who's that?" he asked me.

"My ride." I smiled as Robert strode over and grabbed me by the elbow. Muckle jumped up around his legs, barking like crazy, but Robert ignored him.

"Come," he said, his voice deeper and more manly than usual. "We have to go. I can't live another moment without you by my side, my raven-haired beauty."

I rolled my eyes. Even Robert's vivid imagination had to stretch to refer to me, with my frizzed-out medium-dishwater locks, as a "raven-haired beauty." Still, he'd rescued me from Jamal's awkward boyfriend question, so I was willing to play along.

"I'm coming," I said, allowing him to drag me over to the car with Muckle still leaping around our legs. I waved at Jamal as Robert hurried around to the driver's seat. "See you on Tuesday!"

I barely had time to see Jamal raise his hand to wave back before Robert threw the car into gear and peeled out across the parking lot. Muckle was so excited by all the action that he jumped right into Robert's lap, still barking like a crazy dog.

"Down, foul beast," Robert told him, but he didn't sound that annoyed. I could tell he was in a good mood. He usually was after a successful shopping spree.

"So where'd you get the monkey suit?" I asked, dragging Muckle over onto my lap.

"Second Chance Threads," Robert replied. "Scored some excellent finds. I'll show you the rest later." He glanced over at Muckle, who'd gone quiet and was only wiggling a little bit as he looked out the window. "How was puppy reform school?"

"Great." I settled back in my seat with a smile. "Muckle did okay. Oh yeah, and I just met the love of my life."

Chapter ✿ Five
The next day

ome on, don't be a wuss," Robert said. "At least try it on."

"I'm afraid to," I retorted. "I might get polyester poisoning."

We were in my room, where Robert had just spread all of the previous day's purchases out on my bed, including the one he was currently trying to convince me to put on. It was a hideously slinky teal-blue polyester dress that looked like it should have come with a disco ball. Even Muckle had taken one look at the thing and dashed out of the room.

Robert had arrived at my house wearing the dress's companion outfit—a shiny, geometric-patterned vintage leisure suit. He'd matched it with his favorite pair of purple Converse high-tops and a pair of designer sunglasses he'd probably swiped from his dad.

"Just do it," he urged me. "I want to see if it fits."

"Seriously, I'm not in the mood." I grabbed the slimy half-chewed bone Muckle had left in the middle of the floor, depositing it in his toy basket. "Right after we got home from puppy class yesterday, Muckle got up on the counter and ate the pork chops that were supposed to be thawing for dinner, and Mom totally freaked out. What if the classes don't work? Mom and Dad said if Muckle doesn't start behaving better soon, he's out of here."

"You've only had one class so far," Robert reminded me, fingering his wide lapels lovingly. "Even Mr. and Mrs. Uptight can't be that impatient. Give it a chance."

I sighed. "I guess you're right. But seriously, what if the class doesn't work?"

"What if, what if?" Robert mocked me. "What, are you turning into your sister, Ms. Type A?"

I rolled my eyes. I was so not like Britt, not even a little bit. Still, the insult snapped me out of my pity party. Just the way Robert had known it would.

"Fine," I said, reaching for the disco dress. "I'll try it on. But I'm definitely not leaving the house in this thing."

The dress was so slippery I dropped it the first two times I tried to put it on. By the time I'd gotten it on and adjusted, Robert had picked out a pair of shoes to go with it—some goofy white platforms he'd bought for me at a yard sale over the summer. They weren't easy to walk in, but I managed to toddle over to the full-length mirror on the back of my door.

"Wow," I said, turning this way and that. "This thing actually looks pretty cool. Disco forever!"

I struck a pose, and Robert wolf-whistled. We were debating whether some sparkly purple eye shadow would be overkill (me: yes; Robert: overkill? What's that?) when I heard my mother shouting my name. Uh-oh. That couldn't be good.

She burst into my room a few seconds later. "Lauren!" she snapped. "I thought you promised to keep an eye on that dog. I just found him in the mud room closet, chewing up my Babolat!"

That was one of her tennis rackets. Mom had been a top player in college, and apparently had big plans to go pro before she slipped on an icy sidewalk and messed up her knee. After the surgery she was never the same, though she had taught lessons on the side to help support herself back in her single days. In fact, that was how she'd met my dad—his sister had been one of her regular students.

Muckle himself appeared at that moment, looking very pleased with himself as he slipped between Mom's legs and trotted over to me with his tail wagging. The taste of catgut and graphite must have agreed with him.

"Sorry," I said, snatching him up and hugging him to me. "He's probably just bored. Totally my fault. I'll take him for a nice, long walk right now, and he'll be fine."

I kicked off the platforms, slipped on a pair of flats, and hurried past Mom, who was muttering something about how her beloved racquet wasn't fine. Robert followed me down the stairs.

I paused only long enough to grab Muckle's leash off the hook before continuing out the front door.

"So I can't get you to leave the house, but you'll do it for that stupid mutt?" Robert said.

That reminded me what I was wearing. "Oh, man." I glanced down at myself. The dress looked even shinier in the sunlight. "If anyone recognizes me in this, I'll never be able to show my face in the this town again."

"Here. These will help." Robert grabbed his dad's sunglasses, which he'd tucked into his shirt while I was primping. He stuck them on my face and stepped back. "Perfect. Totally incognito."

"Aren't these men's sunglasses?" I tilted my head, and the glasses slid halfway down my nose.

"Gender is merely a construct." Robert eyed Muckle, who was sniffing at a nearby flowerbed. "I have an idea. Get in the car."

"What? Didn't you hear my mom? I need to tire out this puppy before he eats the rest of the house." I tugged on Muckle's leash to keep him from chewing on Dad's prize rosebush.

"I know. And I have an idea for a way to do that."

"The dog park?" I guessed. "I heard there's one over in Springdale, but I've never been there."

"No, this is way better. Just trust me, okay?"

I shrugged. Maybe it would be better to get Muckle farther away from Mom than a mere walk could take us. "Okay. Come on, Muck."

A few minutes later Robert made the turn into the shopping

center where PetzBiz was located. "Ta-da!" he said. "I'm dying to check out Mr. Hottie McIrish. Since we're in disguise already, I figured we could sneak in and spy on him. You said he's teaching classes here this afternoon, right?"

Drat. Why had I told him that? I'd spent half an hour the night before online-stalking Adam's teaching schedule, but that didn't mean I had to tell anyone.

"We can't," I blurted out. "What if Adam sees me?"

"What if he does?" Robert countered. "You look hot in that dress. And this Adam guy sounds just plain hot."

"I know, but—"

"But nothing," he cut me off. "How often does a guy like this drop into your lap? You need to go for it, Lauren. Seriously. It could be the next best thing to actually dating Corc himself." He smirked. "Besides, if I can pair you off with this guy, that leaves Corc all for me."

"Yeah, dream on. You're not exactly his type, if you know what I mean." I glanced at the store, a flicker of nerves making me shiver. Maybe Robert was right. Maybe I needed to be brave, grab life by the throat, go for it.

Or maybe not. Either way, Robert wasn't waiting for me to make up my mind. He was already getting out of the car.

I did the same. Part of me was terrified by this whole plan, but the rest of me was eager to catch another glimpse of Adam. He was so perfect, I was half-afraid I'd imagined him the day before. I figured it was possible. Muckle might have gotten a little too excited on our way into the store, yanking me into a tall display of canned cat food. One of the cans could have bounced off my head, rendering me unconscious and hallucinatory.

It could happen, right? So maybe it was better to go in there and confirm that Adam was real. I'd even have Robert as a witness this time.

There wasn't much to do on a Sunday afternoon in our boring little suburb, which meant a lot of people were browsing the dog toys and hamster pellets. A few of them glanced curiously at our outfits, but mostly everyone ignored us. That was the fate of being a teenager in suburban America. You were mostly irrelevant, incidental, invisible.

"Wait. We need a plan," I hissed, grabbing Robert's polyester sleeve. "I don't want Adam to see me dressed like this."

"You should. That dress is very eye-catching." He looked me up and down critically. "Although I don't know why you ditched the platforms. And we should have done your hair."

Muckle had been trailing along more or less obediently at the end of his leash. But just then he spotted a greyhound walking by. His ears pricked and he let out a series of piercing yips, dancing around, trying to pull me toward the other dog.

"Quit it, Muckle," I said, distracted by the idea that Adam was so close. "We're supposed to be undercover. No barking."

Luckily, the greyhound completely ignored Muckle and soon disappeared around the corner with its owner. Muckle settled down and started sniffing at the nearest shelf display, which happened to be a stack of puppy piddle pads. I pushed my oversize sunglasses farther up my nose and gave a tug on his leash, then followed Robert toward the back of the store.

We stopped at the end of the aisle closest to the training ring. Peering around a display of toenail clippers, I felt my heart skip a beat.

"There he is," I whispered in Robert's ear.

"Nice!" he hissed back, leaning out a little farther for a better view.

Adam was teaching a class of four adults. The dogs looked like adults too. There were a couple of shepherdy-looking mutts, a golden retriever, and a big poodle with a close-cropped black coat. All of them were walking briskly in a circle at their owners' sides, stopping when they stopped and turning when they turned.

"Wow," I whispered. "They're pretty good. Guess Adam must know what he's doing, huh?"

"Who cares? Just look at him," Robert whispered back, his eyes gleaming with interest. "You have impeccable taste, Parker."

"I know, right? He's super dreamy." I smiled as Adam called for his students to stop. All of them—dogs and humans alike—halted promptly and turned to face him.

Adam started talking to them, but his back was to us now, and I couldn't hear what he was saying. But the dogs' handlers were nodding and smiling.

I was smiling too. Adam was everything I'd thought he was and more. If anything, he looked even better today than he had yesterday. Probably because his gorgeousness had taken me by surprise then.

"He's so your type, Lauren," Robert murmured. "It's hard to hear the accent from here, though. Let's try to get closer."

"No!" I blurted out. "We can't—he'll see us!"

"No, he won't. He's totally distracted." Robert took a step out into the open, straightening the lapels on his jacket. He wasn't exactly inconspicuous in that leisure suit; one of the handlers in the ring was already glancing at him.

"Get back here!" I hissed as loudly as I dared. "Seriously, Robert. If you embarrass me right now, I swear I . . ."

My voice trailed off. I couldn't think of a threat dire enough. Besides, Robert wasn't listening. He was strolling closer to the ring, hands in his polyester pockets, pretending to be very interested in the freestanding display of collars and leashes near the entrance.

I held my breath as Adam glanced toward Robert. Robert smiled and nodded, then busied himself with the leashes. Adam returned his attention to his students, and I let out the breath. At least Robert hadn't said anything to him. Yet.

All this time, Muckle had been busy scratching a particularly itchy spot on the side of his head. Growing bored with that, he stood up, shook himself from head to toe, and trotted past me toward the training ring.

"Muckle, no," I whispered urgently, tugging on the leash.

Muckle completely ignored me. He'd just spotted the dogs

in the ring. His ears went up, his tail wagged, and his entire body quivered.

I winced as he leaped forward, barking at the top of his lungs. Disaster! Darting after him, I grabbed my puppy and hustled back into the shelter of the aisle before Adam could turn around. He might not recognize me in my crazy disguise and sunglasses, but I was sure he'd recognize Muckle as soon as he laid eyes on him.

Robert dashed over to join us. "Danger! Danger, Will Robinson!" he said.

I had no idea who Will Robinson was, and I didn't care. "We have to get out of here!" I exclaimed.

Hugging Muckle to my chest, I took off down the aisle. My polyester dress flapped around my legs, which gave me the giggles.

"What's so funny?" Robert panted, catching up with me.

"Everything!" I replied, still giggling like a loon.

That made Robert laugh too. "Hurry! If he caught a glimpse of you in that dress, he'll be in hot pursuit," he cried, putting on a goofy accent like someone from an old black-and-white film where they all talk funny.

"No way! We can lose him if we—oof!" I'd just rounded the corner of the aisle and crashed into someone looking at a display of dog toys. "Sorry!" I cried, backing off. Then I gasped as I realized who I'd just almost bowled over. "Jamal! Um, hi."

Jamal stared at me for a second, looking confused. Ozzy, who had been sitting at his feet, jumped up and barked happily. Then Jamal's expression cleared.

"Lauren?" he said. "Is that you?" He looked me up and down, and this time it wasn't so much a checking-me-out kind of look as a what-the-heck-is-she-wearing kind of look. "Uh, nice dress."

"Thanks." My face flamed, and I glanced over at Robert, who had stopped next to me. "We're just, you know, goofing around."

Jamal looked at Robert too, and his face fell. "Oh," he said. "Hi. I'm Jamal Hughes—Lauren and I are in the same puppy class."

"Robert James Chase, at your service." Robert swept into a dramatic bow. "And I'm so glad you appreciate Lauren's frock. I'm her personal shopper, and I had to twist her arm to get her to wear it. She looks hot in it, no?"

Jamal blinked, looking confused again for a second. He glanced from Robert—and his outfit—over to me, and back again. His face cleared, and he smiled.

"Really great to meet you, Robert," he said. "And yeah, Lauren looks awesome. Do you do all her shopping for her?"

"No, he doesn't." I rolled my eyes, trying not to blush at the compliment. "Robert just likes to try to bully me into making a fool of myself in public as often as possible."

Robert grinned. "Guilty as charged. But don't let her fool you, Jamal. She loves it just as much as I do. She's a closet extrovert."

"A closet extrovert? Isn't that, like, a contradiction in terms or something?" Jamal asked.

"Maybe." Robert shrugged. "Anyway, what do you think of

today's ensemble?" He pronounced the last word the French way, twirling around to give Jamal a better look at his leisure suit.

"You don't have to answer that," I told Jamal, glad that he didn't seem too freaked out by any of this. Robert tended to frighten some jock types. "Like I said, we're just goofing around. We call it the Disguise Game."

"The what?"

"The Disguise Game." Robert stopped twirling and told him all about it, with me joining in on some of the details. Jamal seemed amused by the whole thing.

While we were chatting, the two puppies were getting reacquainted as well. Ozzy was mostly sniffing Muckle's rear, while Muckle wiggled happily and tried to circle around to get a few sniffs in too.

"So I guess you're probably wondering why Ozzy and I are hanging around here when there's no puppy K today, huh?" Jamal said, glancing down at the dogs.

Actually, the question hadn't even occurred to me. But I nodded.

"It's the Oz man." Jamal grimaced. "He's not really catching on to the whole housebreaking thing. Seems to think the carpeting in the upstairs hallway is the perfect place to do his business. My mom and stepdad are running out of patience."

"No way!" I felt a weird rush of relief. "So Muck and I aren't the only ones with that problem, huh? If he pees on Mom's favorite rug one more time, she's probably going to have a stroke."

"You're definitely not the only ones." Jamal sighed. "It's a good thing Rachel told me about the puppy class. Because this is pretty much the last chance for Ozzy."

"Muckle too," I admitted. "My parents were already losing patience, but last Tuesday was the final straw. . . ."

Chapter ❖ Six
Five days earlier

L auren! Is that you? Get in here!"

I swung the front door shut and glanced at Robert. "Uh-oh. Mom doesn't sound happy."

Somewhere in the house, I could hear Muckle barking. And barking. And then barking some more.

"Should we make a break for it?" Robert suggested.

I slung my school bag onto the mahogany bench in the front hall. "I'd better go see what Muckle did this time."

It was becoming a familiar scene. Muckle would do something naughty. Mom and/or Dad would yell at me. I would promise to keep a closer eye on him. Rinse, repeat.

As we headed toward the kitchen, Mom hurried out to meet us, her Chanel heels click-clacking on the hardwood hallway floor.

"That dog of yours." She jabbed a manicured finger at me. "It's driving me crazy!"

"What happened?" I was still distracted by Muckle's continued barking. He always barked a lot, but this was nonstop.

"The Van Tuyls are having their house painted." Mom paused to wince as Muckle let out a particularly piercing howl.

I nodded. I'd noticed the painters hard at work on the neighbors' house on my way in. "So?" I prompted.

"So what do you think?" She folded her arms and glared at me. "That ridiculous dog has been barking out the window at the painters all day."

"Oh." That did sound annoying. "Did you try distracting him with one of his bones or something?"

"No, I did not." Mom was sounding more annoyed by the second. "I'm not your dog's babysitter, Lauren. When we agreed you could get a puppy, you swore it would be no trouble at all. But it's not turning out that way."

I wondered why she hadn't just gone out to lunch or something to get away from the barking, if it bothered her that much. But I didn't quite dare ask. Not when she was in that kind of mood.

"In any case, this has really set me back," Mom went on grimly. "I was supposed to spend the day making phone calls for my charity banquet. But obviously I couldn't call people with that racket going on in the background. I didn't get a thing done all day, and now I'm way behind."

"Sorry," I said meekly.

"Me too." Mom was still glaring. "You need to deal with this, Lauren—make sure it never happens again. Otherwise, the dog will have to go."

"What?" I squawked. "No! What do you mean?"

"I mean I can't live like this." Mom rubbed her temples. "We're already making sacrifices so you can have a dog as it is."

With great effort, I avoided rolling my eyes. I knew what she was talking about—Britt. Now that Muckle was living in our house, that meant Britt couldn't live there anymore. Whenever she came home from college for vacations and such, she would have to stay in the guest suite over the garage and minimize her time in the main house.

"I know," I said. "But Muckle's part of the family now! I can't give up on him. Especially after waiting my whole life to get him!"

"Your father's not thrilled with the situation either, you know," Mom went on as if she hadn't even heard what I'd just said. "The puppy chewed up his favorite slippers last week, and before that it dug up all the bulbs he'd just planted."

"I know. And I'm sorry—I offered to pay for the slippers as soon as I get enough money, okay?" I winced at the thought. Dad had expensive taste in slippers. "Anyway, I'll take Muckle out for a walk right now, okay?"

"Fine." Mom still sounded worked up. "But we're going to continue this conversation later, Lauren. We can't go on like this."

"Okay." Hurrying past her, I followed the sound of Muckle's yips and found him in the bay window in the dining room. He was standing with his front paws on the glass, staring out the window with his tail wagging in time with each bark.

"Wow, he's got some serious lung power for such a small dog," Robert commented, leaning against the door frame.

I grabbed Muckle, which actually shut him up for a moment. He wiggled in my arms, his warm little tongue washing my chin eagerly. Despite the serious situation, I couldn't help smiling and hugging him.

"Come on, Muckster," I said. "We've got to get you out of Mom's sight for a while, or you're going to drive her over the edge." I glanced at Robert. "Can we go to your place?"

"Sure, I guess." Robert jingled his car keys. "Let's jet."

Robert's family lived a couple of miles from mine in a much fancier neighborhood. His house was easily twice the size of mine. It had a huge, manicured lawn with an iron fence around it. I let Muckle loose to run around out there, and soon he was happily rolling in the grass and leaping at butterflies.

Robert and I leaned against the front porch railing to watch. "What am I going to do?" I moaned.

"What do you mean?" Robert asked.

"What do you mean, what do I mean? I mean about Muckle!" I sighed loudly. "You heard Mom. She's totally fed up. And my dad's not much happier, what with the slippers and the flower bulbs and everything."

Robert patted my arm. "Don't stress about that. I'll pick him up a new pair of slippers next time we hit the mall. He likes the leather open-back kind, right?"

"Right. Thanks," I said. "But that's not really the point. I don't want them to kick Muckle out of the family, but if he doesn't start behaving better . . ."

"Oh." Robert didn't look particularly concerned. "Well, maybe they're right. Having a puppy does seem like kind of a hassle. We're always having to rush right home from school so you can walk him, and I can't even remember the last time we went to the movies."

I barely heard his complaints, which he'd made many times before. I was distracted by watching Muckle frolic in the sunshine, nipping playfully at a blowing leaf. My eyes filled with tears at the thought of losing him. He'd only been mine for a few weeks, but I already couldn't imagine life without him.

Robert glanced at me and raised an eyebrow. "Hey," he said. "You're actually upset about this, aren't you?"

"Of course." I swiped my eyes with the back of my hand. "I mean, just look at him! He doesn't even know what might happen."

Robert regarded Muckle dubiously. Then he shrugged.

"Fine," he said. "If it's important to you, it's important to me. So let's figure out how to deal with this."

I brightened slightly. When Robert set his mind to something, he usually accomplished it.

"Really?" I said. "You'll help me?"

"What are best friends for?" He slung an arm around my shoulders and gave me a quick hug. Then he headed for the door, all business. "Okay, grab the mutt and come inside. We need to do some research."

Soon we were in his massive bedroom, which his parents' decorator had decked out in tasteful shades of beige and taupe. That had been way too boring for Robert, of course, but he'd livened things up with multiple Skerrabra posters on the walls, along with various cheesy vintage afghans, pillows, and even a genuine lava lamp. I sat down on the rug and started tossing a rubber bone to keep Muckle occupied, while Robert grabbed his laptop and flopped onto the four-poster bed.

"Okay, so the first thing we have to do is hire a dog trainer," he said as his fingers flew over the keyboard. "Someone to whip Muckle into shape so he stops being such a doggy hoodlum."

"A dog trainer?" I stood up and peered over his shoulder. "That sounds expensive."

"Not necessarily." Robert clicked on a link, and the PetzBiz logo popped up. "Look, there are beginner group classes right here in Maple View." He scanned the screen, nodding along with what he was reading. "Sounds like that'll be better anyway. It says it lets you socialize your puppy while you both learn."

"Hmm. That does sound good." I'd read lots of stuff on the Internet about how important it was to socialize a puppy with people and other dogs while it was young. I'd been trying, but so far Muckle's socializing was slow going. My parents mostly yelled at him or pretended he wasn't there, and Robert wasn't much better. The only dog Muckle had spent much time with so far was our across-the-street neighbors' elderly bullmastiff, who mostly snoozed in the sun and ignored the puppy jumping all over her. I'd been planning to take him over to the dog park in a neighboring town, but so far Robert had been busy every time I wanted to go, and without a car, the trip would involve a long bus ride with a transfer.

Robert clicked on another link. "We're in luck," he declared. "There's a special class just for handlers between the ages of twelve and eighteen. And a new group starts this coming Saturday!"

"Really?" My heart lifted. That was a lucky break for sure. Maybe my life with Muckle wasn't doomed after all!

Then my heart sank again as I saw the price. I'd spent most of my savings on Muckle himself, then pretty much cleaned out the rest of it paying for his vet checkup, his food, and various other items like collars and toys.

"Forget it," I said with a sigh. "No way can I afford a class right now. Maybe we can find some free do-it-yourself dog training tips on the web."

Robert looked up at me. Then he glanced at Muckle.

"Hey!" he said sharply. "Is that my good boar bristle brush he's chewing on?"

"Muckle! No!" I cried, hurrying over and prying the hairbrush out of the puppy's mouth. It was slimy but still intact. I inserted the rubber bone back in the puppy's mouth, then tossed the hairbrush to Robert. "Sorry about that."

"Yeah. Listen, I think I'll loan you the money for that puppy class." Robert wrinkled his nose in distaste as he deposited the brush on his bedside table. "You can pay me back whenever. And then buy me a new brush."

"No way! Are you sure you want to do that? Thanks!" I was surprised. Oh, sure, Robert's parents gave him plenty of cash, and he was always super generous about sharing it. Exhibit A? All the Disguise Game outfits he'd bought me over the past year and a half.

Still, I hadn't wanted to ask him for any money to help with Muckle. He just hadn't seemed that into the whole idea of me getting a dog, so it didn't seem right.

But hey, if he was offering now, I wasn't going to give him the chance to change his mind. Not with Muckle's whole future at stake. We quickly signed up for the class online, using Robert's American Express card to reserve our spot.

When it was official, I picked Muckle up and hugged him. "Say thank you to your uncle Robert, sweetie," I cooed into his fuzzy ear. "Just you watch—we're going to turn you into a good doggy citizen yet!"

Chapter ✺ Seven
Back to the present

I was so busy telling Jamal the sad saga of Muckle's fall from grace that it wasn't until I'd finished that I realized Robert had slipped away in the middle of my story. That was weird. Usually he seemed to enjoy discussing how naughty Muckle could be.

Then again, he'd heard the whole sordid tale before and been there himself for quite a bit of it. Besides, he didn't have the longest of attention spans. I figured he'd probably just sneaked off for another glimpse of dreamy Adam. I could only hope he wasn't doing something embarrassing like writing my phone number on Adam's arm.

"So anyway," I said, realizing I'd been rambling on at Jamal for quite a while, "that's how we ended up here. Robert and I started researching training classes on the Internet last week, and this puppy class popped up."

"Cool," Jamal said. "Lucky timing, huh?"

I nodded, glancing at Muckle. He and Ozzy had found a piece of dirty old twine on the floor and were playing tug-of-war with it.

"I hope it works," I said. "It could be Muckle's last chance to change my parents' minds."

"I'm sure it'll work," Jamal assured me. "Ozzy's walking on the leash a little better already, even after only one class. Besides, Adam knows what he's doing. Rachel's been filling me in, and it sounds like he's the resident dog freak at MVHS."

"Oh yeah? So did she know him before she signed up for the class?" I was eager for any tidbits of information I could get about my future boyfriend.

Jamal didn't answer. He was looking past me. He smiled and lifted his hand in a wave.

I glanced back, expecting to see Robert returning. I was almost blinded by what I saw, though it wasn't due to Robert's shiny polyester outfit. Because it wasn't Robert coming toward us. Not hardly. It was Adam!

All the blood instantly drained out of my body. At least that was how it felt. I started shaking and was pretty sure I might be about to hyperventilate. I'd never actually hyperventilated before, but there was a first time for everything, right?

"Hey, Adam," Jamal said, clearly not noticing that he needed to call an ambulance for me immediately. "What's up?"

"Hi, guys." Adam looked even hotter when he smiled. Especially when he smiled at me. "Fancy meeting you two here. Couldn't stay away, huh?"

"What can I say?" Jamal joked. "I was craving the smell of liver snaps." He grinned. "Seriously, though, Ozzy loves coming here, and he was getting a little hyper at home, so . . ."

Adam nodded, his expression suddenly going all focused and serious. "They need so much mental stimulation at this age, along with physical exercise," he said, bending to rub both puppies' heads and ears as they leaped up on his legs. "It's great that you're thinking about that, Jamal. So what about you, Lauren? How's Muckle doing?"

As he turned to face me again, his expression went all perplexed. Clearly he'd just noticed my outfit.

"You're probably wondering why I'm dressed like this, right?" I blurted out, quickly scanning my mind for some reasonable-sounding excuse. "Um, it's not exactly my usual dog-walking outfit, if you know what I mean." I laughed weakly.

Just then Robert appeared around the corner of the aisle. He saw Adam standing there, and one eyebrow shot up.

As he came closer, I grabbed him by the arm. "This is my friend Robert," I told Adam with what I hoped was casual chipperness. I gestured at his outfit. "We're both, uh, in the theater club at County Day Academy—that's where we go to school. We just left our rehearsal for, um . . ." Out of ideas, I shot Robert a desperate look.

"*Disco Inferno*," he said smoothly, giving Adam his most winning smile. "It's a musical."

I had no idea if that was a real show, but Adam seemed to buy it. Meanwhile Jamal's expression changed from startled to confused to amused. I could only imagine what he was thinking, since I'd just finished explaining the real reason Robert and I were dressed like time travelers who'd just arrived from 1978. Somehow, though, I didn't relish the idea of telling Adam about the Disguise Game. It just seemed too . . . immature, somehow.

"Anyway," I said, ready for a quick change of subject, "Muckle and I are doing fine. We really enjoyed yesterday's class."

"Good." Adam looked pleased. "It seems like a good group. I think we'll all learn a lot together. It's so important for people to get off to a good start with their dogs—so many puppies miss that early training that sets them up for happy lives, just because people don't know any better. This early socialization is so valuable. . . ."

He kept talking like that for a while, though I stopped taking in the exact words. I was too busy staring at his face, memorizing every angle and eyelash. It was perfect. He was perfect. Even the tiny cowlick in his dark hair was perfect.

After a few minutes, Muckle decided he was tired of playing with the twine. He leaped onto Ozzy with a wild puppy growl, and Ozzy responded by jumping away. Muckle tumbled to the floor, yanking the leash right out of my hand. To be honest, I'd forgotten I was holding it.

As usual, it took Muckle about a tenth of a second to realize he was free. I lunged for the leash, but I was way too slow. The leash handle slithered away from me like a snake, and with a yip of triumph, Muckle took off down the aisle at top speed.

"Muckle, no! Get back here!" I hollered. Remembering that Adam was still standing there, I quickly added, "I mean, come, boy! Come!"

Muckle completely ignored me. Of course.

"Guess the training hasn't really taken hold yet, huh?" Robert observed calmly, leaning against the display shelf.

"Come on," Adam said to me. "I'll help you catch him."

"Thanks." Leaving Jamal struggling to hang on to Ozzy, who clearly wanted to join in the chase, I took off after the runaway puppy. Adam was right behind me.

We chased Muckle up and down several aisles. He managed to stay just ahead of us, though he paused now and then to pull toys or snacks off the shelves. A few other customers tried to head him off, but he was too quick for them, dodging outstretched hands and darting around legs and shopping carts and other dogs.

"Quick—you go that way, and I'll circle around," Adam directed as we came to the end of another aisle.

I obeyed, jogging around the corner. Muckle was already halfway down the next aisle, though he'd stopped again to sniff at some bags of kitty litter.

"Muckle!" I called. "Stop right there!"

At that moment, Adam appeared at the far end of the aisle. He let out a soft whistle, and Muckle's ears pricked curiously. He trotted a few steps toward Adam, then stopped and sat down.

Adam sat down too. I crept closer, wondering if I could lunge forward fast enough to grab him. Seeing what I was doing, Adam looked me in the eye and shook his head slightly.

I froze. Muckle was standing again. His tail wagged slowly as he took another few steps toward Adam.

"Here, buddy boy," Adam crooned, grabbing a bright blue plastic kitty litter scooper thingy off the shelf beside him and waggling it at the puppy. "Come on, let's play, okay?"

Muckle barked twice, then rushed forward. I was afraid he was about to give us the slip again, but instead he starting jumping all over Adam, tail wagging and tongue flapping.

Adam laughed, rolling on the floor with Muckle for a moment before scooping him up and climbing to his feet. "Got him!" he called to me with a grin.

I hurried toward them. Adam set Muckle down and handed me the other end of his leash.

"Thanks so much," I said breathlessly. "I guess Robert's right—we haven't exactly made a ton of progress yet."

"It's all right. Like I told you guys yesterday, puppies aren't born knowing how to behave." Adam leaned over and rubbed Muckle's head. "We have to teach them what we want. That's the only way we can all live together peacefully, eh?"

I nodded like a bobblehead. Everything sounded great in that accent. At that moment Muckle spotted a shih tzu walking past at the end of the aisle. He barked and leaped toward it, and I barely tightened my grip on the leash in time to prevent an embarrassing rerun of the action we'd just finished.

"Oops," I said, my cheeks going hot. "Down, Muckle. I mean heel." I tugged on the leash. Muckle completely ignored me.

Adam smiled. "Here, let me show you a few tricks," he said. "We'll cover this in class soon. If the pup isn't paying attention to you while you're walking, you can't just scold him. Puppies don't understand English, yes?"

"Muckle does," I replied. "Seriously. He can hear the word 'dinnertime' from a mile away."

Adam chuckled. "I hear you. But just humor me, all right? Walk down the aisle with Muckle. If he starts to wander off to the right, you need to turn abruptly to the left. Don't say anything to the dog—just do it. You want to surprise him, eh? Now give it a try."

I wasn't quite sure what he wanted me to do. It was distracting to be instructed by someone so hot, especially now that all his focus was on me, with no other class members to share the spotlight.

Still, I gave it a try. "Come on, Muck," I said, walking down the aisle. Muckle almost immediately turned to look at something on the shelf, and I yanked on the leash.

"No, not like that." Adam hurried over. "Here, let me show you."

He put his hand on the leash right above mine. His arm grazed my arm, and our shoulders bumped. Once again, I thought I might hyperventilate. He was touching me! As in actual skin-to-skin contact!

I surreptitiously scanned the surrounding area, wondering if Robert was watching this. He was down at the far end of the aisle with Jamal, waving his arms around and chatting in his usual animated fashion.

Good boy! It was pretty obvious that he was running interference, playing the wingman, making sure I had this moment with Adam all to myself. I was grateful, but I didn't dwell on that for long.

"Okay, let's try this again. . . ." Adam walked me through the leash-training exercise, showing me how to surprise the puppy and keep him guessing so his attention was more likely to stay focused on me.

As for me? All my attention was focused on Adam. His hands were gentle as they guided mine, and he smelled good up close, with only the slightest whiff of doggy odor.

Or was that me? I had a moment of panic before I decided it didn't matter. We were in a pet supply store—everything here had a doggy odor. Besides, Adam loved dogs. Maybe I should start bathing in Eau de Puppy Breath.

Okay, being that close to Adam was making me a little giddy. And I'd barely said a word to him so far. I knew I had to pull it together if I didn't want this magical moment to go to waste.

"So—um, how'd you learn so much about dog training, anyway?" I asked as he finally stepped away, allowing me enough space to breathe semi-normally again.

He shrugged and smiled. "I've always loved dogs—we always

had a pack about the place when we lived in Ireland. Guess I have a bit of a knack with them. That's what everybody says, anyhow."

"Cool. So do you have a dog of your own?"

I guess that was a stupid question, but he didn't seem to mind. "Three of them, yeah," he replied. "Couple of border collies and a Jack Russell terrier. I do agility and some obedience with the girls, and the terrier is a flyball fiend."

"Oh, I've heard of that stuff," I blurted out. See? My Internet research in preparing to get a puppy had come in handy! "Agility's that obstacle course thing, right? That looks like fun."

"I bet Muckle would think so too." Adam smiled at my puppy, who was sitting still for a change, gazing up at Adam adoringly. Like puppy, like owner. "You ought to try it with him once he's got his basic training down. Actually, I teach a couple of beginner agility classes, plus take on some private students. I can give you the info if you think you might be interested."

"I'm definitely interested." Understatement of the year.

Adam's smile widened. "Good. I like an enthusiastic student." Suddenly his smile wavered, and he checked his watch. "Speaking of which, I just remembered—I'm supposed to be meeting a client over at the dog park in fifteen minutes, and it takes twenty to get there. I've got to go."

He actually sounded . . . disappointed. Could it be? Was he as reluctant to leave me as I was to see him leave?

No, probably not. But if he was even a tiny bit reluctant, I'd take it.

"Okay," I said. "Thanks for the tips. And for helping me catch my little monster."

"Anytime." He bent to ruffle Muckle's fur, which made the puppy leap around in ecstasy. "See you in class, Muckle." He straightened up and directed that megawatt smile at me again. "You too, Lauren."

"Okay." I didn't want this to end. "Um, actually, I'm on my way out too. I'll walk you."

"Sure." Adam glanced at Robert and Jamal, still barely visible at the far end of the aisle. "What about your friends?"

"Um, they're going somewhere after this. Without me." Not wanting him to ask any more questions, I decided to switch us back to a safer subject. "So these private lessons—how often do you teach?"

We chatted about his dog training schedule for the short walk out of the store. Realizing it would be pathetic to actually follow him to his car, I stopped on the sidewalk.

"Okay," I said, holding tightly to Muckle's leash. "See you Tuesday."

"For sure." He lifted one hand in a wave. "Later, Lauren."

"Bye." I bent down and pretended to fiddle with Muckle's collar so I had an excuse to stay right there, watching as he went striding out into the parking lot. He climbed into a beat-up beige minivan—not exactly the rugged Range Rover type of vehicle I would have imagined he'd drive, but whatever—and drove away.

Only then did I head back inside. I found Robert browsing the magazine rack near the registers.

"How'd it go, lover girl?" he asked with a smirk.

"Great. Tell you after we get out of here." I looked around. "Where's Jamal?"

"He took off after you went outside with your hot new boyfriend." Robert shrugged. "Guess he was jealous."

"Ha-ha, very funny." I wasn't really focused on Jamal. I just wanted to make sure he wasn't going to wander up and interrupt once I started telling Robert about my Adam encounter.

"You know, he actually isn't the macho jock type you'd take him for at first glance," Robert said.

I blinked. "What are you talking about? Adam isn't the jock type at all."

"I'm not talking about Adam," Robert said. "I mean Jamal. I only started talking to him to keep him out of your hair, but he's actually a pretty cool guy."

"Sure, he's great. Maybe you two can go antiquing together sometime." I snorted, then grabbed his hand and dragged him toward the door. "Now let's get out of here so I can tell you all about Adam. And then start figuring out what I should wear to puppy class on Tuesday."

Chapter ● Eight
Tuesday, 1:45 p.m. and counting

When did school get so freaking boring?" I muttered to Robert as we walked out of English class on Tuesday afternoon.

"It was always boring. You're just noticing now?"

Robert shuffled through his backpack—a vintage leather number he'd picked up on eBay. "Shoot, I forgot my science stuff. Walk me to my locker?"

"Yeah, okay." I trailed along after him. Every time I had to dodge a group of obnoxious jocks elbowing one another like Neanderthals, or a pack of expensively dressed prepsters slouching along as if they owned the planet, I found myself wishing I were at MVHS instead. Sure, there were probably plenty of jerks there, too. But at least there I'd have a chance of spotting my own personal Prince Charming in the halls.

Speaking of halls, County Day Academy was located in a historic building right in the middle of what passed for a downtown in Maple View. That meant it was on the small side as schools went, with the lockers to match. I rarely bothered to leave more than my gym clothes and a couple of granola bars in mine. Actually, that was pretty much all that fit without squishing.

But Robert hated getting his constantly rotating collection of designer bags and backpacks all distended with too many books, so he insisted on shoving stuff into his locker on a daily basis. Which could make it a challenge to get anything back out at times.

"Did you finish the lab write-up last night?" he asked as he shuffled through the locker.

"The what?" I wasn't really listening. I'd been trying to figure out exactly how many minutes were left until that afternoon's puppy class started.

He smiled. "Ah, young love. It turns the brain to mush." He chucked me under the chin. "Seriously though, Lauren, it's nice to see you falling for a real-life Prince Charming for a change—especially since he happens to come with a hot accent. To be honest, the unrequited Corc thing was getting a little tired."

"Does that mean you're tired of him, too?" I challenged.

He smirked. "Not a chance. But we're talking about you, sweetie. Like I said, it's good to see you out there. Going for it. Flirting your pretty little head off."

I snorted. "Flirting? Me?"

"What do you think you were doing the other day?" Robert

lifted one eyebrow knowingly. "Trust me, I recognize flirting when I see it."

I couldn't argue with that. Robert was definitely a romantic at heart—much more so than I was, actually. He was all about the meaningful glance, the first kiss, the happily ever after. All those sappy chick flicks he was always dragging me to were proof enough.

Still, I wasn't about to admit to anything when he was looking so smug. "I don't know what you're talking about," I told him. "I don't even know how to flirt."

"I beg to differ," he retorted. "So does Adam, I'm sure. And Jamal, for that matter."

"Jamal?" I blinked at him. "Okay, I might concede your point when it comes to Adam. But I was definitely not flirting with Jamal."

Robert slammed his locker door shut. "Maybe you should try it sometime," he said. "He's almost as hot as Adam. No accent, of course, but the rest of the package is there—he's cool, he's smart, he's more age appropriate...."

I stared at him, waiting for the punch line. But there didn't seem to be one. Was Robert crazy? Jamal was cool and all, but he was no Adam.

"Are you nuts?" I said. "I just met the man of my dreams, and you're already trying to hook me up with some other guy?"

"Sorry." Robert hoisted his backpack onto his shoulder and checked his watch. "I'm just saying, if things don't work out with

Adam, it's nice to have a backup. But I'm sure things will work out with Adam," he added hastily, probably catching the murderous glint in my eye. "He's totally perfect for you. He's like Corc, only even better."

"Better than Corc?" I asked, slightly mollified. I didn't know where the whole Jamal detour had come from, but I wanted to get back on track.

"Yeah, totally." We started wandering toward our next class. "He's younger than Corc, for one thing. And available—no supermodels to compete with."

"Always a plus," I agreed.

"And then there's the job," Robert went on. "Tagging along on those world tours would get awfully old after a while, don't you think?"

"Of course." I grinned at him. "You're right. Adam's perfect."

The bell rang, sending us scurrying off toward the science lab. I only hoped I wasn't so distracted by my daydreams about Adam that I accidentally blew up the school. Not that I'd miss the school, mind you. But I didn't want anything to make me late for puppy class.

After school, Robert and I stopped by his house first so he could change clothes. Then we swung by my house to pick up Muckle. He was waiting for us when I opened the front door, his entire fuzzy little body quivering with excitement. Mom was waiting too, and she was also quivering. But in her case, it was with irritation.

She wanted to tell us all about how naughty Muckle had been that day, but luckily, I had an excuse to duck most of her complaints this time.

"Sorry, Mom," I said, snapping the leash onto Muckle's collar while he leaped around joyfully, trying to lick my face. "We don't want to be late for puppy class."

She frowned. "Yes, I suppose that dog needs all the class time he can get." Then her gaze wandered to Robert. "What are you wearing, young man?"

Did I mention that Robert had stopped to change clothes? He was flying solo in the Disguise Game that day, all decked out as a summer tourist even though it was almost November. A pair of oversize Bermuda shorts put his pale, knobby knees on full display. His second-favorite Hawaiian shirt—the one with luau scenes all over it—flapped over a white patent leather belt. A pair of antique binoculars hung around his neck, and the whole outfit was topped off with a wide-brimmed hat.

"What, this old thing?" Robert shot Mom an innocent smile as he twirled on our front step. "It was a little warm in school today, so I thought I'd slip into something more comfortable."

"Hmm." Mom turned away, clearly losing interest in Robert's latest fashion statement. "Make sure you're home in time for dinner, Lauren."

When we arrived at PetzBiz, Robert got out of the car and pulled his hat lower over his face. "Ready to go incognito," he said.

I sighed. "Must you? I mean, are you sure you don't have any important shopping to do at the Goodwill store? It's drop-off day, you know."

For a moment he looked tempted. Then he shook his head.

"I want to be there for you, Lauren," he informed me. "Keep an eye on things. Watch your back."

"Whatever." I knew better than to try to talk him out of it. The more I'd try, the more stubborn he'd get. And the more likely to pull something embarrassing.

As we reached the front door, I heard someone calling my name. Muckle spun around, yipping joyfully as Rachel and Gizi hurried toward us.

"Hey!" I greeted her. "Ready for today's class?"

"I hope so." Rachel sounded a little breathless. "I took Gizi for a long walk right after school so she'd maybe be calmer." She glanced at her puppy, who was leaping around doing the crazy-puppy-happy-welcome dance with Muckle. "I'm not sure it worked."

I smiled sympathetically. Every time I saw Gizi, I was reminded that Muckle could be much worse. "This is my friend Robert," I said. "Robert, this is Rachel. She goes to MVHS."

"Robert James Chase, at your service," Robert said with his usual bow and flourish.

"Rachel Kardos." Rachel smiled shyly, clearly not quite sure what to make of Robert. He got that a lot. "Hi."

Robert tossed a salute in my general direction. "I'm off. Have fun, kids."

He hurried off, disappearing behind a stack of birdcages. "Where's he going?" Rachel asked.

"Who knows." I rolled my eyes. "But don't be alarmed if you notice him spying on our class. Robert can be strange at times, but he's mostly harmless."

Rachel smiled uncertainly. "So how's Muckle doing?" she asked. "Have you guys been practicing the stuff Adam taught us?"

"Of course." I could feel my face heating up as I remembered that extra private lesson on Sunday afternoon. But I wasn't about to tell Rachel that. "I think Muck's finally starting to catch on to the whole walking-on-a-leash thing. At least sometimes. Sort of."

She laughed. "I know what you mean. One step forward, two steps back, right?"

"Yeah. And then ten steps off to the side, chasing a squirrel." I was a little distracted, since I'd just spotted Jamal coming. Ozzy was turning himself inside out, he was so obviously happy to see us. To be honest, Jamal looked pretty psyched too. His smile lit up his whole face. Not that I was noticing things like that about him.

Quickly scanning the surrounding area, I was relieved to see that Robert was nowhere in sight. Although he could be hiding somewhere, of course. Probably peering through his binoculars and giggling over seeing me with Jamal. I frowned slightly as I thought about my best friend's comments earlier. Where had he gotten the idea I was flirting with Jamal? That I'd ever flirt with

Jamal? The guy was cool—and okay, anyone with eyes could see that he was good-looking—but he was so not my type. Even without Adam in the picture, there was just no way.

"What's up, ladies?" Jamal said as he reached us. "I was afraid I'd be late—I had to stay after school to talk to my cross-country coach about next weekend's meet."

"Nope, you're right on time." Rachel smiled at him. "Should we head back to the training area?"

"Sure. Let's go." I hurried off, practically dragging Muckle away from his delighted greeting ritual with Ozzy. If my cheeks were going pink because of stupid Robert's stupid comments, I didn't want the others to notice and wonder. Especially Jamal. He was a nice guy, and I didn't want to give him the wrong impression.

As soon as we started class, I forgot all about Jamal, Robert, and everything else. Even my own name, probably. Because Adam was just as amazing as ever. He was energetic, he was knowledgeable, he was totally focused on the dogs. We started by reviewing some of the stuff we'd done in the first class. Just your basic sit, down, walk on a leash. Most of the puppies seemed a little better today, though the hound mix was just as hopeless as ever, and Ozzy kept getting distracted by Jamal's shoelaces.

As for Muckle? He started off okay and performed his sits like a champ. But while we were walking, a bird flew overhead. Yes, a bird. I could only assume it was a wild sparrow or something that had mistaken the cavernous store for some kind of natural cave and found a way inside, since the store didn't sell any live animals except fish.

And that was all she wrote. The other dogs didn't even notice the bird. But Muck started jumping around, head pointed skyward—well, ceilingward—barking like a loon.

"Lauren." Suddenly Adam was at my side. "Having some trouble over here?"

"Sorry." I was all too aware of his eyes boring into me. His body, so close to mine. I wanted to reach over and run my hands through his shock of raven hair, but I held back. "Um, he's just a little distracted."

"Can I try?" He reached out.

For one giddy moment I almost put my hand in his. I realized just in time that he was actually reaching for the leash. I handed it over, trying not to shiver as our hands touched briefly.

"Okay, Muckle," Adam said, bending down to caress the puppy's fuzzy head. "Let's show them how it's done, eh?"

Then he straightened up and walked to the center of the ring. And what do you know? That disloyal little beast trotted along beside him, in almost perfect heel position, as if he'd been doing it all his life. Figured.

"All right, everyone," Adam called out to the entire class. "Let's stop and sit and watch for a moment. I'm going to demonstrate a few things with Muckle here. . . ."

He went on to do exactly that. And what do you know—once

again, the Muckster was a superstar! Oh, I wouldn't claim he was perfect. But he seemed to turn into a whole different pup with Adam at the other end of the leash.

It was amazing. It was awe-inspiring. It was hot.

Suddenly something clicked into place. Up to that point Adam had fit right into my usual type in some ways—the hair, the eyes, the accent. But he'd been an anomaly in others. I'd always gone for artsy guys. Singers like Corc, various actors, the occasional hip-hop dancer or whatever.

But now I realized something. The thing they'd all had in common wasn't being artsy so much as it was having a passion for something, whether that something was music, acting, or dance. That was what had attracted me to them, given them that certain something I couldn't resist. And by that standard, Adam fit right in. His passion was dogs, and he had a real talent with them—just as he'd modestly mentioned the other day.

The thought made me feel a tiny surge of optimism. And not only about my (potential) love life, either. With Adam helping me, maybe Muckle wasn't a lost cause after all. Maybe he could work his magic, turn things around, make Muckle's behavior acceptable even to my über-picky parents.

Before I knew it, Adam was calling an end to that day's class. Where had the time gone?

"One more thing," he said as we started to gather up our stuff. "I forgot to mention it last time, but I wanted to tell you about the dog park over in Springdale. It just opened this past summer, and it's a very cool place. They definitely created it with dogs and dog owners in mind. There's agility equipment, private runs for smaller dogs, all kinds of stuff. I suggest you all check it out if you can. Because remember—a tired dog is a good dog." He smiled. "Maybe I'll even see you there—I take my dogs all the time. Okay, good class, everyone! See you on Saturday."

He turned away and fiddled with the paperwork on his chair. Jamal clipped on Ozzy's leash, then leaned toward me. "That dog park sounds pretty cool, huh?" he said.

"Definitely," Rachel said, looking up from adjusting Gizi's harness. "Maybe we should all take a field trip sometime."

Jamal grinned. "Sounds like a plan."

"Yeah." I was too distracted to focus much on the chitchat. Excusing myself, I hurried over to Adam.

He glanced up at my approach. "Hey, Lauren. Good work today." He smiled and ruffled Muckle's ears. "Your pup made a perfect demo dog."

"Thanks." I cleared my throat. "That's, um, what I wanted to talk to you about. I want to thank you for showing me how good he can be. I guess I just assumed he'd always be too hyper to really learn much."

Adam chuckled. "Spoken like a first-time puppy owner," he said with a twinkle in his eye. "Don't fret, Lauren. Muckle is a terrific puppy. He's supersmart and trainable, with a very sweet temperament. With the right guidance, he could go far in dog sports."

"You mean like we were talking about the other day?" I said. "Um, agility and stuff?"

"Exactly." Adam picked up his papers and tucked them under his arm, then turned to face me. "You really should consider getting him started in that, Lauren. Try some beginner lessons, see how he likes it."

"Sounds good." My heart was pounding. Was it my imagination, or was he gazing at me super intently? "Um, but I'm not sure where to start."

His smile broadened. "Well then, it's lucky you know me. I'd be happy to help you out. Like I was saying the other day, I teach lots of beginners to love agility just as much as I do." He winked. "Dogs and owners."

I was pretty sure I was blushing. Somehow, though, I didn't mind. Adam and I were connecting. I could feel it. The feeling made me bold.

"That sounds amazing," I said, tilting my head in what I hoped was a flirty way. "I'd love it. So when can we get started?"

"As soon as Muckle graduates from puppy K," Adam replied. "But hey, there's no reason you can't start getting him used to the equipment, maybe testing his interest a little. Like I was just telling the class, the Springdale dog park has everything you need. My dogs and I practice there a lot, and I teach some private clients there who don't have their own equipment. It's great."

I held my breath, suddenly sure he was about to invite me

to go to the dog park with him. For a dog-crazy guy, that would totally count as a date, right?

"Adam?" The pug's owner barged over, dragging her puppy behind her. "I have a question. Puggsly still jumps up on me, and I can't figure out how to get him to stop. . . ."

I could have killed her. But the damage was done. The magical moment was gone, shattered into a zillion pieces. All I could do was smile once more at Adam, give a tug on Muckle's leash to pull him away from the pug, and head out to find Robert.

Chapter ●Nine
TGIF

When the final bell rang on Friday, I was out of my seat like a shot. I hurried to my locker, then to Robert's. He was peering into the small mirror he'd taped inside the door, fiddling with his hair. He was still doing the eighties-angst-rocker thing with it, though the exact style seemed to evolve slightly each day.

"Ready to go?" I asked.

He continued to stare at himself. "Go where?"

"The dog park. I told you about it at lunch, remember? I figured we could swing by and pick up Muckle, maybe stop off for a snack at that taco place on the way to Springdale. . . ."

"Sorry, no can do." Robert finally tore his gaze away from his own reflection, glancing at me and then swinging the locker door shut. "I told my dad I'd play tennis with him this afternoon."

"What?" That stopped me in my tracks. The only thing that had helped me survive the boring day at school was imagining today's trip to the dog park. Including the strong possibility of running into Adam. Thanks to my Internet stalking, I knew he didn't teach any classes at PetzBiz on Friday afternoons. And the way he'd been talking the other day, it had sounded as if he spent every spare moment at the dog park with his dogs. It didn't seem like foolish optimism to hope I might run into him there.

I tried to explain some of that to Robert. But he just kept shaking his head.

"Look, you know I'd rather hang with you than the fuddy-duddies at the country club," he said. "But Dad is demanding some face time, and I don't want to be cut out of the will."

"Fine." I wanted to argue, or maybe just throw a tantrum. But what good would that do? "Maybe we can go another time."

"Sure, maybe. Come on, I'll drop you off on my way home."

When I let myself into the house a little while later, I found my mother in the front hall rifling through the mail. Muckle was nowhere in sight when I entered, but he came running a few seconds later, flinging himself at me as eagerly as if we'd been parted for seven years instead of seven hours.

"That beast has been incorrigible all day," Mom informed me, glaring at Muckle over the tops of her rhinestone-encrusted reading glasses. "He never sits still."

"Yeah, about that." I wasn't ready to give up on my afternoon plans yet. "I was going to take him to the dog park in

Springdale to run off some energy, but Robert's busy. Can you drop me off?"

Mom checked her watch. "Actually, I'm leaving for a meeting over in Madison in ten minutes. I suppose I could swing through Springdale on the way. You'd have to find your own way home, though."

"That's okay. I can take the bus." I tried not to grimace at the thought. Our local suburban bus line wasn't exactly state of the art. There were only a handful of buses, all of them old, smelly, and slow. But a girl had to do what a girl had to do, right? Besides, riding the bus would be another good socialization exercise for Muckle. At least that was what I told myself.

I felt a shiver of nerves as Mom pulled her Lexus to the curb half an hour later. "Is this it?" she asked, peering at the tall iron gate.

"Yeah, I think so," I said with a straight face, even though the gate had foot-high letters spelling out community dog park on it. "Thanks for the ride."

I checked to make sure Muckle's leash was attached to his collar, then got out of the car. Muckle jumped out after me, spinning around in circles like he always did in a new place.

As my mom pulled back into traffic, Muckle and I headed into the park through the big iron gate. It was a beautiful autumn day, warm and sunny with a slight breeze, and it seemed everyone in the tri-county area was out enjoying the weather. That definitely included the dog park. There had to be at least two dozen dogs in there of all shapes and sizes.

"Come on, Muckie," I said, tightening my grip on the leash. I could already tell Muckle was revved up by all the new sights and sounds. "Let's check it out."

We wandered around, getting the lay of the land. Well, I wandered—Muckle dashed back and forth in front of me, growing more excited by the second.

No wonder. There was a lot going on. We started by checking out the huge central lawn, which took up about two-thirds of the place. It was vast, flat, and grassy, with only a couple of large shade trees breaking things up. Tons of dogs were running around out there. Some were wrestling in groups of two or three, while others focused on the owners tossing Frisbees or tennis balls.

Muckle was getting overstimulated just watching all that action. I wasn't about to let him loose—I'd probably never be able to catch him again. Or at least not before the buses stopped running at midnight. So we headed over to the shadier area along the perimeter. It was divided into different sections. There were a bunch of smallish pens where little dogs were playing, along with a couple of slow-moving large dogs that I guessed were too elderly to handle the rough-and-tumble of the main park. The area also contained water stations, poop deposit cans with plastic bags for anyone who'd forgotten to bring some, and even a couple of crates where people could temporarily stow their dogs.

"Oh, look," I told Muckle as we passed the last of the small pens. "This must be the agility stuff."

We'd come to another separate pen, this one much larger than the small-dog playpens. It was dotted with colorful equipment, only some of which I knew the names of. There were jumps, ramps, weave poles, a seesaw, and more. At the moment a cute mixed breed was practicing running through a fabric tunnel, his eyes focused on the twentysomething woman directing his movements. Both owner and dog seemed to be having fun. On the sidelines, an older woman was leaning against a tree trunk and watching while her dog—a tiny, delicate-looking papillon—chewed busily on a toy bone.

I glanced at the gate, which had shut behind us after Muckle and I entered. "I guess it would be okay to let you off your leash for a while," I told Muckle. "You can't do much damage in here, right?"

Muckle sat relatively quietly as I clicked the leash off. Then he immediately dashed off, smelling along the fence line.

After a moment he spotted the papillon. Muckle's tail went straight up, and his ears pricked. Letting out several sharp barks, he bounded toward the tiny dog.

The papillon's owner looked over, her eyes widening in alarm. "Stop!" she yelled at Muckle, waving her arms. "Stay away!"

The way she was acting, you would have thought there was a giant hungry lion charging toward her instead of a friendly sheltie puppy only slightly larger than her own dog. Still, I didn't want to cause trouble on our first visit, so I decided to humor her.

"Muckle!" I called. "Come back here!"

But the dog park was clearly way too much for Muckle's tiny brain. He barked again—his hyper bark, the one that meant his brain had pretty much switched off—and started chasing the papillon around and around its owner's legs. The woman shrieked, trying to grab her dog. For some reason the papillon seemed to regard both its owner and the crazy-eyed larger dog as equal threats. It dodged the woman's flailing arms, then raced off toward the big A-frame obstacle, heading up and over with surprising speed and, well, agility. Muckle followed, his claws scrabbling on the brightly painted wood.

"Sorry!" I cried as I ran past the woman. I tried to catch Muckle as he leaped down the last few feet of the A-frame, but he dodged me easily. "I'm really sorry," I called over my shoulder. "He's friendly, he just gets too excited sometimes."

"You have to stop him! He's going to hurt Midgie!" The woman sounded frantic.

Once again, I nearly rolled my eyes. But people were starting to stare. The young woman with the mixed breed had stopped her dog atop one of the pieces of agility equipment, and on the other side of the fence a sporty-looking girl with short blond hair had also stopped to watch. Beside her was a pretty red-and-white-spotted dog—I was pretty sure it was a Brittany, though I wasn't focused on playing Name That Breed at the moment.

"Don't chase them," the blond girl called out. "You're just egging them on."

Easy for her to say. I gulped, not sure what to do. The papillon was still managing to keep at least a yard or two ahead of Muckle. Not for lack of trying on Muck's part.

"Lauren? Everything okay?"

It was Jamal. He was standing outside the gate with Ozzy. I'd never been so glad to see a friendly face.

"I can't catch him," I blurted out, my eyes filling with tears. "He's not listening to me at all, and this lady's worried about her dog, and . . ."

Jamal was already letting himself in. "Here. Hold Ozzy's leash," he said, shoving the loop into my hand.

Then he reached into the pocket of his letterman jacket and pulled out a tennis ball. He let out a sharp whistle, then wound up and threw the ball. It bounced off the grass—just inches in front of Muckle's nose.

Muckle skidded to a stop, his eyes following the ball as it bounced again. With a short bark, he turned and chased after it.

"Midgie! Come here, baby!" The woman hurried forward and grabbed her dog as it slowed down, cradling it to her chest. With a glare at me, she hurried out of the ring.

Meanwhile the woman with the mixed breed grabbed Muckle as he pounced on the tennis ball. I hurried over to retrieve him, thanking her profusely as she handed him over.

"Maybe we should get Muckle and Ozzy into a pen of their own," Jamal suggested.

"Good idea." I held my puppy tightly as we let ourselves out of the agility ring. Muckle was still pretty worked up, and I didn't want to take any chances of him getting loose in the larger area of the dog park.

The blond girl, who was probably around my age or a little older, was still watching from outside. "Everything okay?" she asked. "Cute sheltie, by the way."

"Thanks," I said, not slowing down as I followed Jamal toward an empty pen nearby. The girl seemed friendly, but I wasn't in the mood for socializing at the moment.

Once all four of us were safely in the pen, Jamal shut the gate firmly behind him and then unsnapped his dog's leash. I set Muckle down on the grass, and the two puppies joyfully greeted each other.

"Thanks," I told Jamal as we watched them play. "You totally saved us—I think that woman was about to call the cops on Muckle. How'd you know what to do to stop him chasing that dog?"

Jamal shrugged. "Ozzy will stop anything to chase a ball," he said. "He loves it more than anything. I was hoping Muckle might be the same way."

Sure enough, Ozzy's ears pricked at the word "ball," and he stopped what he was doing and raced up to his owner, panting eagerly. I smiled and patted him.

"I'm not sure Muckle's as obsessed as that," I said. "But he is easily distracted. The important thing is, it worked."

"Yeah." Jamal pulled the tennis ball out of his pocket again and tossed it across the pen. Ozzy raced off after it with Muckle in hot pursuit. Jamal shot me a sidelong grin and flexed his arm playfully. "I gave up baseball back in middle school when I discovered running, but I guess I've still got it."

I laughed. "Definitely. If I'd tried to throw the ball like you did back there, it probably would've hit Muckle in the head. Or no—with my luck it would've hit the lady with the pap!"

He chuckled, then cocked his head. "Pap?" he echoed.

"Papillon. That's the breed of that little dog Muck was chasing. You can recognize them by the big ears—they look sort of like butterfly wings, which is how the breed got its name."

"Gotcha. And wow. You sure know a lot about dogs." Jamal leaned back against the iron fence and grinned. "Or maybe you just know a lot about everything. Like that obscure Scottish island you named Muckle after, for instance. Do they teach you stuff like that at County Day or what?"

"Not really. And I definitely don't know that much about dogs, either." I smiled back ruefully. "It's easy to research breeds and stuff online, but this training stuff is another thing."

I glanced at Muckle, who was running in circles around Ozzy as the larger puppy trotted back toward us with the ball in his mouth. Then I shot a look toward the agility pen across the way. The lady with the papillon had disappeared, but the blond girl was in there now, calling out instructions to her dog. Meanwhile the woman with the mixed breed had gone back to work too. Neither dog was paying the least bit of attention to the other, keeping their attention on their owners as they jumped over stuff and zipped through tunnels or whatever like pros. Would Muckle ever be like that? For that matter, would he ever learn to walk on a leash without trying to pull my arm out of its socket?

I sighed. Jamal glanced at me. "What? You look worried. I latched the gate, I swear."

"It's not that. I was feeling pretty good about Muck's progress after Tuesday's class," I told him. "But now I'm back to wondering if he'll ever turn into a good dog."

Jamal looked sympathetic. "I hear you. Ozzy ate one of my mom's magazines last night." Ozzy dropped the ball at his feet, and he threw it again. "Mom was furious. Mostly because he left scraps of slobbery paper all over the house."

"Bummer." I shook my head. "Adam keeps saying they're just puppies, and puppies don't know what to do until we teach them. I don't know why our parents can't seem to understand that and maybe cut us some slack, right?"

"Yeah," Jamal said. "But in my case, I know why. My folks didn't really want to get another dog after our old dachshund passed away. I had to talk them into letting me get a puppy."

"Sounds like my parents."

"Yeah. Rex was really old when he died, and he was pretty cranky the last few years." He shrugged. "Actually, he was always pretty cranky. We started calling him T. Rex because he was always trying to bite people. Looking back, I realize it's probably because we never taught him any better."

"Sounds like something Adam would say." I tried not to look too lovesick at the mention of his name.

"Right," Jamal agreed. "Anyway, Rex was pretty much untrained. But I want to do it right this time. I had it all figured out—I'd go to the shelter and find some tall, lean dog that could keep up with me whether I was doing a long run or a sprint."

I watched Ozzy as he grabbed the tennis ball in his mouth and tossed it up, leaping after it. He was definitely athletic, but the words "tall" and "lean" weren't the first to spring to mind.

"So what happened?" I asked.

"Well, first my friends tried to change my mind about what to get," he said. "My girl-crazy cousin Reggie thought I should pick out something small and fluffy and cute. He says that kind of dog is a girl magnet." He grinned at me. "So what do you think? Is it true?"

I had the uncomfortable feeling that he was flirting with me. But I tried to sound casual as I replied, "I don't know. Maybe you should take a poll of all the girls you can find. That's another way to meet them, right?"

That made him laugh. "Anyway, that was Reggie. My friend Kenny had the opposite opinion. He wanted me to get a big dog— something tough-looking and macho."

I looked over again at Ozzy, who was neither big and tough nor cute and fuzzy. "So how'd you end up with Oz?"

"When I went to the shelter, there was just something about him. Yeah, he's not much to look at, I guess. He's sort of scruffy and gangly and looks like three different dogs put together." He shrugged. "So I don't know. He just has, like, a good energy, you know? We got along right away. Plus, I could tell he was active enough that he'd be able to keep up with me while I run, even if he wasn't exactly what I was picturing."

I couldn't help being impressed. Most of the guys I knew at school were all about the optics. Who had the snazziest car, the best clothes, the prettiest girlfriend. That was the main reason I had zero interest in getting to know most of them—and didn't mind that it seemed to be mutual. Took it as a compliment, almost.

But Jamal didn't seem to be that way at all. Was it a public school vs. private school thing? Were people just less shallow at MVHS? I tended to doubt it—I'd gone to public school up through eighth grade and didn't remember it being that much different.

So maybe it was just him. In any case, hearing him talk about choosing Ozzy made me feel a bit sheepish about the reasons I'd chosen Muckle. But never mind. It had worked out for the best—I was crazy about the little monster now, regardless of his breed.

Ozzy and Muckle had stopped chasing the tennis ball to wrestle, but now Ozzy bounded toward us with the ball in his mouth again. He dropped it at his owner's feet and barked. Jamal scooped up the slimy ball and tossed it in one graceful motion. Nice.

Wait, why was I noticing that? I wasn't interested in him that way. Maybe being in love with Adam was making me more sensitive to male beauty in any form.

"I guess it's a good thing we both found Adam, right?" I said, my mind now wandering in that direction. I shot a surreptitious look around the rest of the dog park, but my future boyfriend was still nowhere in sight. "Um, so you were saying you had a study hall with Adam once. Do you know him well?"

"Nope." Jamal bent to grab the ball again as Ozzy brought it back. "I mean, the school's pretty big, and he's a senior. We don't really hang in the same crowd, you know? But I've seen him around. Didn't know he was into dogs until Rachel told me, though."

I recalled him saying that before. Even though I was itching to ask more questions, I held back. For one thing, it didn't sound as if Jamal would be able to answer most of them, since he didn't know Adam much better than I did. For another thing, I didn't want him to think I was some crazy stalker. After all, Jamal had no way to know about that spark that had passed between Adam and me the other day. He'd probably just see me as a pathetic girl with a crush on the teacher.

Jamal hurled the ball across the enclosure again, sending both puppies zooming off after it. "So what's your story, Lauren?" he asked. "I know you like obscure Scottish bands and dressing up as a disco goddess, but what else do you do for fun?"

Uh-oh. That sounded an awful lot like flirting. And while it was flattering to think such an amazing guy might be interested in me, I didn't want to let him think I was interested back. Not in that way. I wanted us to be friends and leave it at that.

So I scanned my mind for something about me that would turn him off. Something that made most guys look at me like I had two heads. Aha . . .

"Horror movies," I blurted out. "I love 'em. The bloodier the better."

"For real?" His eyebrows shot up in surprise.

I smiled. Mission accomplished. An admission like that should put me squarely in just-one-of-the-guys territory.

"Awesome! I love horror flicks!" Jamal's face broke into a big grin, and he raised his hand for a high five. "See? I knew you were cool as soon as I met you! So what are some of your favorites? Do you get into the classics—you know, Hitchcock, Romero—or mostly newer stuff?"

I returned the high five weakly. "Um, pretty much all of it," I said. "Except I usually wait for the new ones to come out On Demand or whatever, because Robert hates scary movies. He's always dragging me to sappy romances and stuff."

Jamal chuckled. "Robert seems like . . . a character." He hesitated, sneaking me a sidelong glance. "So are you guys, you know, best friends, or what?"

Despite meeting Robert, he still seemed to want confirmation that our relationship wasn't romantic. As if. And yeah, by the way, mission obviously not accomplished. This wasn't a problem I was used to having, to say the least, and I wasn't sure how to handle it.

But it was clearly way too late to go back to pretending that Robert and I were a couple. "Yeah, we've been best friends since I started at County Day last year," I said. "I met him on my first day, at lunchtime. . . ."

Chapter ● Ten
One year and two months earlier

I skulked over to the empty end of a long table in the far corner of the cafeteria. The nonempty end was filled with a bunch of freshman boys arguing over some sports event. The cafeteria at County Day Academy was a lot smaller than the one at MVMS, which meant it was hard to find a spot to be alone.

And I definitely wanted to be alone. My first day at private school wasn't going well so far. I'd figured it would be easier making friends and fitting in at a smaller school, but that wasn't turning out to be the case. Everyone here appeared to have known one another since kindergarten, if not before. And they didn't seem interested in getting to know someone new. Nobody even said hello when I stumbled into my homeroom after spending twenty minutes searching for it, too intimidated to stop anyone to ask for help.

For the rest of the morning, I'd wandered around silently and listened to my new schoolmates fill each other in on their fabulous summers, most of which seemed to involve foreign travel and copious amounts of sunscreen. I wasn't about to tell any of them that I'd spent the past three months helping Mom stuff envelopes for her latest charity thingamajig. Not that anyone asked.

Then came lunch. I'd been dreading it all day, and not that delicious the-killer-is-coming dread I loved so much in horror movies. No, this was a sick pit-of-the-stomach dread, the kind that said I was going to spend my high school career alone, scurrying around like a mouse on the edges of people's consciousness. Oh well, maybe at least the teachers would grow to like me.

As I dumped my lunch bag on the table and sat down, I noticed a guy walking toward me. He was well dressed, but in a different way from most of the guys at County Day. Skinny pinstriped pants, slicked-back hair, funky red shoes. There was only one word for it: dapper.

I watched his approach warily out of the corner of my eye, pretending to be very busy unwrapping my sandwich. What did he want? Was he coming to tell me this table was reserved or something?

"All my other best friends have been blond," he announced, sliding into the seat across from me. "You'll be the one to break the curse."

I blinked. "Huh?"

He stuck out his hand. "I'm Robert. Robert James Chase. You're Lauren something-or-other, right? The new girl."

"Yeah." I stared at his hand for a moment before realizing he wanted me to shake it. I did so, tentatively. "Um, hi. Lauren Parker."

Robert slung a battered suede messenger bag onto the table. Flipping open the flap, he pulled out a stainless steel bento box and a bottle of Orangina.

"This stuff is super popular in Europe," he said, noticing me staring at the drink. "It's my new thing. I only eat and drink stuff from other countries. I'm like the opposite of a locavore."

Okay, this guy was definitely odd. But he seemed friendly, which was more than I could say for most of my new school-mates. Besides, "odd" had never bothered me. I'd been the only one who would talk to the weird Russian exchange student at my old school.

"So what's wrong with blondes?" I asked Robert.

His head snapped up. This time, I could tell I'd surprised him. "Pardon me?"

"What's wrong with blondes? You said I'd be breaking the curse."

He stared at me for a long moment. Then he grinned. "Busted," he said. "There's nothing wrong with blondes. Some of the greatest women in history have been blond—I mean, Marilyn Monroe, right? Grace Kelly. Madonna."

"I read somewhere that the real-life Cleopatra was actually a blonde," I supplied.

"Exactly." He sipped his Orangina. "So maybe I shouldn't have called it a curse. More like a streak. I'm just in the mood for a change of pace." He winked at me. "And I have the feeling you're it, Parker."

Chapter Eleven
Back to the dog park

heard a clock striking four somewhere in the distance beyond the dog park. It was only then that I realized I'd been chatting with Jamal for a long time. After telling him about how Robert and I had met, we'd moved on to other subjects. Jamal had asked me about my family and told me about his. His mother was an anesthesiologist at the local hospital, and—surprise!—his dad worked for the same pharmaceutical company as mine, though in a different building.

I was surprised to learn that Jamal wanted to be a doctor like his mom. "Really?" I said when he told me.

I guess I must have sounded a little too surprised, because he grinned. "Yeah, I know. My friends all tell me I'm too laid-back to make it through med school. But I'm actually pretty serious about it. I mean, I still make Mom take me to the hospital with her on

Take Your Kid to Work Day, even though the cutoff is supposed to be, like, age twelve."

I laughed. "Sorry, I wasn't doubting you. It's just not what I would've guessed. Besides, I have no clue what I want to do when I grow up. I'm actually impressed."

Just then the puppies ran over. This time Muckle had the ball. Ozzy was bounding back and forth, trying to snatch it away from him. Muckle dodged the other puppy, then dropped the ball between me and Jamal.

Jamal laughed. "See? Muckle really is trainable. Ozzy just taught him to play fetch!"

I smiled and reached down to grab the ball. Jamal bent to pick it up at the same time. His hand ended up on mine, both of our fingers wrapped around the slimy yellow ball.

I froze. I guess he did too. Because he kept his hand there for what felt like an hour, though it was probably only a second or two. Anyway, it was enough time for me to notice that his skin was warm, and that he was now close enough for me to smell his shampoo. Or maybe it was aftershave.

"Oh, sorry," he said, finally pulling away.

I yanked my hand back too, leaving the ball on the ground. "It's okay. Um, I should probably get going. I'm pretty sure there's only one bus going my direction in the next hour or two." I grimaced. "Maybe someday this area will get a halfway decent public transportation system, right?"

"You're taking the bus home?" Jamal cleared his throat.

"Listen, I have my car right outside. I could drop you off. If you want."

I hesitated, using Muckle as my excuse not to answer right away. As I chased down my puppy and snapped on his leash, I tried to figure out what to do. On the one hand, I hated taking the bus. On the other hand, I didn't want to give Jamal the wrong idea. Would accepting the ride make him think I liked him as more than a friend?

Then again, he'd offered both Rachel and me a ride that first day after puppy class. Maybe he was sort of like Robert that way—he'd drive anyone anywhere anytime.

Besides, I really hated taking the bus.

"Thanks," I said, dragging Muckle toward Jamal and Ozzy. "That would be great. You know—if you're sure you don't mind."

"No, it's cool." He looked so happy that I almost took it back. "Where do you live?"

I told him my address as we gathered the puppies and headed out of the pen. As it turned out, it was practically right on his way.

"You can even pick the music for the drive if you want," he offered as we walked toward the exit. "I mean, it sounds like you've got way more refined tastes than I do."

I laughed. "I won't argue with that. There's this pretty cool college station that we might be able to—"

Suddenly Muckle exploded into a frenzy of excited barking. Ozzy quickly joined in, both puppies leaping and yanking at the ends of their leashes as they tried to drag us forward faster.

"Whoa, what just got into them?" Jamal wondered.

I didn't answer. I couldn't. Because I'd just spotted Adam walking into the park!

He looked as hot as ever in faded jeans and a black Windbreaker. A pair of intense-looking border collies were trotting beside him. Neither had a leash on, though it was hard to tell, since both dogs stayed in perfect heel position. Adam did have a leash on his third dog—a brown-and-white terrier a little smaller than Ozzy.

Adam spotted us almost immediately. What with the pups spinning around wildly at the ends of their leashes, barking their heads off, we were hard to miss. Even in a dog park.

"Hey, guys," Adam called in that gorgeous accent, his gorgeous face lighting up in a gorgeous smile. "You came to check out the park!"

"We did!" I said in a tone so chipper I even surprised myself.

"Yeah," Jamal added with a grin. "You should've seen Muckle tearing up the agility equipment earlier. So to speak."

"Oh yeah?" Adam said, turning to me.

I blushed. "Um, sort of," I said. "Anyway, are these your dogs?"

The two border collies had sat down on either side of Adam, alert but still. The terrier remained on his feet, his nose twitching as he gazed suspiciously at Ozzy and Muckle.

"Check it out, Oz and your dog could be brothers." Jamal laughed. "Or maybe father and son."

"Yeah." Adam smiled. "I bet Ozzy has some Jack in him. Well,

I'd better get my gang over to the agility pen, see if it's free. You guys on your way out?"

"Yes," Jamal said at the same time I blurted out, "No, not really."

Jamal looked surprised. I turned to him, smiling apologetically.

"I just remembered," I said, thinking fast. "My mom is coming by to pick me up on her way home from her meeting. She'll kill me if I'm not here, especially since she always forgets to check her texts." I shrugged and tossed an *old people—what can you do?* smile at Adam.

"Oh." Jamal hesitated. "Uh, okay. See you both tomorrow in class, I guess."

"Yeah." I gave him a quick wave as he turned to leave. Muckle seemed disappointed to part with Ozzy, but soon comforted himself by sniffing noses with one of the border collies. "Look," I told Adam. "He must know they're both herding breeds, right?"

"Maybe." Adam sounded a little dubious, but he was still smiling. Was he glad I'd stayed?

"So what are you and your dogs going to do today?" I asked. "Are you going to practice agility? Maybe I can watch—you know, figure out if I want to try it with Muckle. If that's okay."

"Sure, sounds good." Adam nodded agreeably. "Let's go, then."

I fell into step beside him. For once Muckle was behaving pretty well. He kept veering over toward Adam's dogs, wagging his tail and sniffing in their direction. But they mostly ignored him.

"Your dogs are really beautiful," I said, glancing at the

border collies. Both of them had glossy black-and-white fur a little shorter and sleeker than Muckle's. One had perfect tuxedo markings, with a white blaze down her face and four white paws. The other had funkier markings, with a mostly white head and one floppy black ear.

"Thanks." Adam smiled. "They're my babies. I've raised all three of them from puppies—Shasta and Lark come from solid working lines with plenty of instinct. . . ."

He kept talking about the dogs' breeding for the rest of the walk to the agility area. I didn't pay much attention to the details, mostly just enjoying the feeling of letting that musical accent wash over me.

When we reached the pen, both of the dog owners from earlier were gone. Instead a stout older man was guiding a lively boxer over some jumps. "Hi," Adam called to the man as he let himself and his dogs in, holding the gate for me and Muckle. "Mind if we join you?"

"Go ahead," the man called back. "We're just about finished."

"Thanks." Adam whistled, and all three of his dogs snapped around to gaze at him alertly. Even Muckle stared at Adam with interest.

"What does the whistle mean?" I asked.

"It's just a signal to pay attention," he said. "They know when they hear it, they're supposed to look to me for further instructions."

"Cool." I stood back and watched Adam put his dogs through

their paces. They demonstrated each piece of equipment, and in between commands Adam explained what they were doing. I barely noticed when the older man left the ring, except that Muckle stopped pulling on the leash trying to go over to say hi to the boxer.

At the end of the demonstration, Adam called two of the dogs to him and commanded them to jump up on the large, flat wooden table at one end of the course. He'd already told me it was called a "pause table," though the first time he'd said it, I'd thought he was saying "paws table," which had made him laugh.

"Down," he told the dogs, making a gesture with his hand. I recognized it—it was the same hand signal he'd started teaching us to use with our own puppies.

The tuxedo-marked border collie, whose named I'd deduced was Lark, instantly sank into a down position. The terrier, whose name was Jinx, sank slowly into a sit first, eyes trained on Adam. After spending time with Ozzy, I was starting to recognize that terriers' minds seemed to work a little differently from those of other dogs. I could almost see Jinx wondering if he really had to lie down.

But on the second command, the terrier obeyed with a sigh, resting his nose on his paws as he lay beside the larger dog. Adam told them both to stay, then turned to face Shasta, the other border collie, who was standing at attention nearby, ears pricked toward him.

"Wait," he told her. Then he turned to me. "Want to see how it all comes together? Shasta and I can show you a course like the one we did in our last competition." He smiled proudly at the dog. "She won that one, by the way."

"I'd love it," I said. "Thanks!"

"Great. Here we go." Adam returned his attention to Shasta. He called her over and told her to sit, then sent her at the first obstacle, a jump. He ran along as she sailed over it, directing her with hand and voice toward the next jump. After that came the weave poles, then the long, narrow dog walk, then various other obstacles. Trainer and dog were in perfect sync the whole way through; Adam barely seemed to have time to name and point at the next obstacle before Shasta was racing toward it.

The course finished with Shasta hopping up on the pause table beside the other two dogs. She sank down immediately, panting with exertion but on alert, as if perfectly willing to run the whole course again.

"Good girl!" Adam cried with a grin, stepping over to fondle her head as she wiggled with pleasure. He stepped back from the table and clapped his hands. "Free!" he said.

Both border collies visibly relaxed; Lark stood and stretched, then jumped off the table and started sniffing around at something in the grass underneath it. Jinx was off the table just as quickly, though Shasta stayed where she was, seeming to enjoy the rest.

"That was so cool," I said, hurrying to join Adam by the table. "I totally want to do that with Muck!"

"Awesome." Adam grinned at me. "I was hoping you'd feel that way. Want to try a sneak preview right now?"

His smile made me feel as wiggly and happy inside as Shasta at the start of her agility course. Was it my imagination, or was Adam gazing at me as if I were the only other person in the world? I couldn't be imagining that, right? In any case, it was definitely a different look than the one I was used to from puppy class.

"Definitely," I said, trying not to shiver too visibly. "How do we start?"

"Here, let me take him for a sec." Adam reached for Muckle's leash, his hand brushing mine and making my skin go all tingly and warm. "Come, Muckle. Let's see what you've got."

Muckle jumped up and barked, clearly excited to be getting some attention. "What do you do first?" I asked.

"It's important to introduce the equipment properly." Adam slipped back into teacher mode, his voice going all serious. "The most important thing is to keep things fun and positive. You want the dog to think agility training time is the most awesome part of his day."

"Even better than dinnertime?" I joked. Muckle's ears pricked toward me at the sound of his favorite word.

Adam smiled briefly, then returned his attention to Muckle. "Okay, little guy," he said in a high, bright voice. "Shall we try a jump? Come on, let's jump!"

He used the leash to guide Muckle toward a low jump, one that hadn't been on Shasta's course. It was too low for Muckle to duck under, so when he came to it, he hopped over easily.

"Good boy!" I exclaimed.

Adam was praising Muckle too, using that same happy, high-pitched voice. Muck lapped it up, his tongue flopping out of his mouth. He let out a few barks and spun in a circle, his tail wagging almost too fast to see.

Adam laughed. "I think he likes it so far, eh?" he said to me. "Come on, why don't you give it a try?"

What followed was probably the most thrilling twenty minutes of my life. Adam stuck to me like glue as I learned how to guide Muckle over a few easy obstacles. At least once at each new obstacle, Adam's hand was on mine, showing me exactly what to do. Once, when we were helping Muckle over the A-frame, he even leaned in over my shoulder so his chest touched my back. It was the next best thing to slow dancing.

"Excellent!" he exclaimed as Muckle crept eagerly but cautiously down the far side of the seesaw as I praised him lavishly. "See? You're both naturals. All you need is a little instruction, and you'll be ready to start entering beginner competitions in no time!"

"You think? Wow." I was flushed and out of breath from running around; I hoped that was making my cheeks turn a pretty shade of pink rather than causing my entire face to go all blotchy. Just in case, I buried my face in Muckle's silky fur as I grabbed him off the seesaw and gave him a big hug. He wiggled joyfully and slurped at my ear.

"Yeah, Muckle definitely has talent. He could eat up the competition in his size group," Adam assured me.

"Wow," I said again, releasing Muckle, who ran off to jump on

Adam's dogs. "Well, it's probably just because you're such a good teacher."

He grinned. "You flatter me. But seriously, I'd be happy to talk about private lessons if you're interested. You and Muckle would be a blast to teach."

"Really?" Now I was sure my cheeks were pink. Probably more like fuchsia. Adam wanted to give me private lessons! He thought it would be fun to spend more time with me, one on one! Well, one on two, technically. But I couldn't think of a better wingman than Muckle, at least where dog-crazy Adam was concerned. "Thanks," I said, cautiously taking a step closer and smiling up at him. "That would be great. Super great."

"Yeah," he agreed, smiling back. "You really think you're ready to put in the time? Agility is pretty addictive, you know."

"Oh, definitely. I'm pretty sure I'm already hooked." Hey, what do you know? This flirting stuff was easier than I'd thought.

"Great." His grin got even wider. Was it my imagination, or was he leaning in toward me? At least a little?

We stood there smiling at each other for a long, breathless moment. I felt incredibly connected to him, as if anything could happen. Maybe even a first kiss . . .

Then my phone buzzed loudly in my pocket, breaking the spell. "Oops," I said, grabbing it and glancing at the text. "That's my mom wondering where I am—I was supposed to start dinner."

A look of confusion passed over his gorgeous face. "Your mum? I thought she was picking you up."

Oops. This was exactly why I didn't lie much. I wasn't very good at it.

"Um, yeah." I thought fast. "That's why she texted, actually. She forgot to stop by and get me. She remembered when she got home and realized dinner wasn't ready or whatever."

It wasn't the smoothest of stories, but Adam seemed to accept it. "So how are you getting home?" he asked. "Do you live close enough to walk?"

"No. Guess I'm stuck taking the bus." I paused, waiting for him to pick up his cue and offer to drive me home.

But he just stepped back and called sharply to Jinx, who was chewing on something over near the gate. Then he looked at me again. "We can talk more about the private training stuff later," he said, sliding back into teacher mode. "Muckle should really get through puppy class first, anyway."

"Oh. Okay." I grabbed Muckle and snapped on his leash. He didn't put up a struggle—he'd had a full day and was starting to run out of energy. For once. "Listen, thanks again—this was fun."

"For sure. Take care, Lauren." He smiled. "See you tomorrow." Then he turned and whistled for his dogs. By the time I let myself out the gate, Lark was halfway through her own course.

Five minutes later I was peering at the sign at the bus stop, trying to figure out how many eons it was going to take me to get home, when my phone buzzed again. This time it was my dad. He'd just talked to my mom on the phone and heard where I was, which was only a few miles from his office. He told me he was leaving work and offered to swing by and pick me up. I texted back, gratefully accepting the offer.

"No bus for us today, Muckety-Muck," I told my puppy, who had collapsed at my feet and wasn't even paying attention to the bird pecking at a crumb on the sidewalk five feet away. "You had fun today, didn't you, little guy?"

Muckle responded with a yawn, and I laughed and ruffled his ears. It really had been quite a day. For a second, I flashed back to my chat with Jamal. But I shook my head, not wanting to waste any brain cells on that; I would need all of them to savor the time I'd just shared with Adam.

I shivered, remembering the feel of Adam's hand on mine, the look in his eyes during that special, breathless moment. We'd tell our kids about this afternoon someday—I was sure of it.

"I had a good time too, buddy," I murmured, leaning back against a lamppost to wait for my dad. "For sure."

Chapter ● Twelve
Saturday, way too early

I was dreaming about being attacked by an angry goose when I was suddenly yanked out of a deep sleep. No, wait, that wasn't a goose—it was my mother. She was standing by my bed, squawking loudly about something.

Squinting up at her, I yawned. "What time is it?" I mumbled.

"Time to get up and clean up after that dog of yours!" she snapped.

Uh-oh. Still fuzzy with sleep, I sat up and rubbed my eyes. What had Muckle done now? He'd been so tired after we got home from the dog park the evening before that he'd fallen asleep in his dinner.

Not me. My afternoon with Adam had left me feeling totally jazzed. Robert's parents had dragged him to some dinner party with friends of the family, so I'd had to wait for him to get home at around eleven to fill him in. We'd stayed on the phone until almost one a.m., discussing every juicy detail.

After that late night, I could have used another couple of hours in bed, but Muckle was now apparently fully rested and terrorizing my mother.

"Ugh," I said as I glanced at the clock. Not even seven thirty. Way too early to be awake on a Saturday, no matter what time I'd gone to bed the night before.

Mom grabbed my robe off the back of my desk chair and tossed it at me. "Rug cleaner. Dining room. Now."

Uh-oh squared. It didn't take much to read between the lines here, sleep deprived or not. Muckle had used Mom's favorite rug as a doggy toilet. Again.

"Sorry," I said through a yawn. "I'm coming."

By the time I'd finished scrubbing puppy pee off the rug, I was too wide awake to go back to bed. Besides, Muckle was dancing around, looking for attention.

"You look like you need more exercise," I told him as I pulled on a pair of jeans. "Want to go for a walk?"

He barked and practically turned himself inside out jumping around. I took that as a yes.

Soon we were out wandering down the block. It was a cool morning, and we had the subdivision sidewalk to ourselves aside from the squirrels, who were busy storing nuts and stuff for the winter. Every time he saw one of the bushy-tailed creatures, Muckle barked and tried to take off after it. And every time, he seemed surprised to be caught up short by the end of the leash.

"I bet Adam's dogs would never try to decapitate themselves over a stupid squirrel," I told Muckle as I held him back from chasing yet another one. "You could learn a few lessons from them, you know."

The squirrel disappeared into the branches of the Smiths' oak tree, and Muckle bounded back to me. Would he ever be as well trained as Adam's border collies?

"Guess the only thing we can do is try, right?" I told the puppy.

His ears pricked and his head tilted with interest as he stared up at me, looking ready for anything. That gave me an idea.

"Sit, Muckle." I made the hand gesture Adam had taught us. "Sit, boy!"

Muckle continued to stare blankly for a moment. Then his little haunches dropped, and he sat.

I laughed. "Good boy!" I cried, using the happy, high-pitched tone I'd heard from Adam. "Good, good boy!"

Muckle leaped to his feet, bouncing around and barking happily. I rubbed his ears, and then we continued our walk.

But thinking about Adam and his dogs—and seeing Muckle sit—had inspired me. This time we didn't just walk. I continued to throw in commands here and there. When we came across a shoe box that must have blown out of someone's trash or something, I even convinced Muckle to treat it like an agility obstacle and jump over it. It took a couple of tries, a few stares of confusion from Muckle, but finally he caught on and sprang over easily. That brought about so much loud, high-pitched praise from me and loud, high-pitched barking from Muckle that Mrs. Levy opened her front door and peered out at us suspiciously.

"Morning!" I called to her with a friendly wave. Then I tugged on Muckle's leash, hurrying us around the corner.

Once we were out of sight, I bent and gathered Muckle up for a big hug. He wiggled and licked my face.

"You really are a good pup, aren't you?" I said. "Adam's right— you definitely have potential." I smiled as I said Adam's name, mentally drifting back to the day before. He truly was amazing— and not only because of the cool accent and the amazing cheekbones and awesome hair. He had actually given me hope that I might be able to train my dog.

Muckle wiggled harder, and I set him down. He jumped around me, looking happy and excited. Sort of like he was waiting for the next fun thing we were going to do.

I grinned at him. "Okay, buddy. Let's see if we can find something else to jump over."

By the time we returned home almost an hour later, Muckle was tired but happy. As I closed the front door and unsnapped his leash, I could hear my mother's voice drifting out of the kitchen.

I wandered that way and found her sitting at the kitchen table with the phone pressed to her ear. When she saw me, she said,

"Hold on a sec, here's your sister," into the phone, then gestured me over. "It's Britt," she told me. "Come say hello."

"Hi," I said into the phone. "How's college?"

"Fine." Even in just one word, Britt managed to sound snippy. "How's the animal? Mom says he tinkled in the house again."

I grimaced. Definitely snippy.

"Muckle is fine," I told her, perching on the edge of a chair and watching as my mother bustled around the kitchen, pretending not to listen to my half of the conversation. Muckle went over to his water dish and took a drink. "His housebreaking is coming along. Did Mom tell you we're taking a puppy kindergarten class?"

"Whatever." Now Britt sounded downright annoyed. "Look, Lauren, if the dog thing isn't going to work out, could you try to make a decision before Thanksgiving break? Because I'm really not thrilled about being forced to stay in the guest house just so I can breathe in my own home."

I rolled my eyes. Clearly my perfect older sister still saw me as some irresponsible little kid. When Mom and Dad had told her they were letting me get a puppy, she'd probably figured I'd lose interest before she came home for break. Like the hermit crabs I got when I was five and ended up giving away to the kid next door.

Well, I wasn't five anymore. And Muckle definitely wasn't a hermit crab.

"Sorry, sis," I said through gritted teeth. "You're just going to have to suck it up, I guess. Because Muckle is here to stay."

Over by the sink, my mother pinched her lips together in that disapproving way she had. But she didn't say anything, or even turn to look at me.

Still, I could read body language well enough. She agreed with Britt. She still thought Muckle might not work out. Which meant I basically had until Thanksgiving—just a little over a month away now—to turn Muckle into the perfect puppy.

But no pressure, right?

"You look awfully cranky for a girl who's supposed to be in love," Robert said as I climbed into the Volvo a few hours later.

"Do I? Sorry." I arranged my features into a placid, pleasant smile. "Better?"

"Fab." Robert shot Muckle a dirty look as the puppy scrabbled at the back of my seat. "So what's going on?"

I told him about Muckle's latest housebreaking accident as we drove out of the subdivision. "Then Perfect Britt called," I added with a grimace. "I think she's working on Mom to make me get rid of Muckle."

"Bummer." Robert didn't sound particularly concerned. "So anyway, let's discuss your strategy for today."

"Strategy?" I echoed, a little distracted by Muckle, who was licking the backseat. Luckily, Robert didn't seem to notice. "What are you talking about?"

"Mr. Perfect, of course." Robert straightened his tie with the hand that wasn't on the steering wheel. His outfit today was fairly subdued—white shirt, skinny pants, funky leopard-print tie. "Now that you've got his attention, you need to keep it," he told me. "Strike while the iron's hot. All that jazz."

He sounded enthusiastic. That made me nervous. Well, more nervous. The closer we got to PetzBiz, the faster my heart pounded. Would Adam act any differently toward me today?

"I don't know," I told Robert. "Maybe I should just play it cool today. Let Adam make the next move. If he wants to." I chewed my lower lip. Something had been bothering me a little, but I hadn't let myself think about it until that moment.

Robert sensed my angst immediately. "What?" he demanded, glancing over.

I sighed. "Well, it's just that the more I think about it, the more I wonder why Adam didn't pick up on the cue to give me a ride home. I know I'm not like a flirting expert or anything, but I don't think I could've possibly made it more obvious."

Robert reached over to fiddle with the radio, which was whispering a staticky version of a recent pop hit. "Some guys are dense," he said. "Way of the world, darling. Or maybe he's shy."

"Shy?" I wrinkled my nose and thought about that. "He doesn't seem shy."

"Anyway, it's the twenty-first century—you don't have to sit around waiting for the guy to make the first move," Robert said. "If you want him, you need to go out and get him!" He smiled. "Luckily, I have the perfect plan."

Uh-oh. Robert's plans tended toward the—how could I put this?—wildly impractical. Like the ones in those screwball romantic comedies he liked so much. Whereas I preferred things a little more direct, like in a horror movie. You know—grab ax, chop up coed. That sort of thing.

"I don't know . . . ," I began.

He didn't let me finish. "Look, Adam already said he'd give you private lessons, right?" He glanced over, waggling his eyebrows suggestively. "So why not invite him over for one—say, tomorrow afternoon?"

"But he said Muckle has to wait until he graduates puppy class to start agility training," I said.

Robert shrugged, gunning the car to make it through a yellow light. "Doesn't have to be an agility lesson. You could ask him to help you with Muckle's housebreaking problem. Kill two birds with one stone."

"I couldn't," I insisted. Then I paused, thinking it over. "Could I?"

"Sure you can." Robert sounded confident. "Don't think of it as asking a guy out. Think of it more like hiring a contractor."

I rolled my eyes. "It's not like I do that every day either."

"Yeah, okay. This doesn't have to be a big deal, Parker. You like this guy, and you're pretty sure he likes you. It's practically a business arrangement."

"Hmm." The more I thought about it, the more the idea was growing on me. Why should I wait around, wondering if Adam actually liked me, if he was ever going to make a move? At the very least I could do what Robert was suggesting, which would be setting things up to let it happen. As Adam himself told us—we had to set our puppies up for success. Give them the opportunity to do the right thing by making it easy for them. Wasn't this sort of the same situation?

"So?" Robert glanced at me, eyebrow arched. "Are you going to do it, or do I need to keep convincing you?"

"No, it's cool. I'm convinced—I think." I took a deep breath. "I mean, what's the worst that can happen, right?"

"That's the spirit."

"No, really. I've got nothing to lose. If he says no or acts weird about it, I can always pass it off as an actual training request thing rather than any kind of date."

Robert frowned. "Wait a minute. If you're going to go for it, you should just go for it." Glancing over at me, he shrugged. "Never mind. Baby steps, right?"

"Right." Spotting the turn for the shopping center, I felt my heart start to pound. "Baby steps."

Class actually went pretty well. Muckle seemed calmer and more focused than usual. He only stopped a couple of times to sniff at things when he was supposed to be walking with me, and when it was time to sit, he was the first one to obey.

"Perfect, Lauren," Adam called out, pointing at us. "I can tell you've been practicing."

"Thanks." I could feel myself glowing as I bent to give Muckle a treat.

"Show-off," Jamal whispered with a grin from his position beside me. Ozzy was frolicking around his legs—sitting seeming to be the last thing on his mind.

I smiled back. "What can I say? Muckle's the teacher's pet," I whispered back. "Get it? Teacher's pet?"

Jamal groaned, but then he laughed. "Remember how you were saying you don't know what to do when you grow up?" he said. "Well, you might want to cross stand-up comedian off the list. Just saying."

I laughed and stuck my tongue out at him. Then I returned my attention to Adam.

Adam kept us so busy that I forgot about Robert's strategy for a while. Well, sort of. By the time class ended, I was feeling as jumpy and distracted as Muckle usually was when I got home from school.

"See you next time, everyone," Adam said as he dismissed us. "Make sure you practice between now and then. Consistency is key."

I kept an eye on him as he headed out of the ring. He stopped just outside and started shuffling through his paperwork. Good. Now was the time to strike.

Before I could head out there, Jamal and Rachel came over. "Hey Lauren, Rach and I were just talking," Jamal said. "We've both been meaning to try out that café over on West Street—it's supposed to be very dog friendly."

Rachel nodded and pushed a strand of hair behind one ear. "I stopped in there with some friends the other day, and there were a bunch of dogs hanging out with their owners. They even sell dog cookies and stuff."

"So what do you say?" Jamal asked me. "Want to go check it out? You can bring Robert if he's around too."

"Oh. Um, sounds fun." I was still watching Adam out of the corner of my eye. "But I can't go today. You guys have fun, though."

Without waiting for a response, I picked up Muckle and hurried out of the ring. Adam glanced up when he heard me coming.

"Hey, Lauren," he said. "What's up?"

"I, uh . . ." Now that I was here, facing my dream guy, my mind went blank. "Um, you know, I was thinking—that is . . ."

He blinked at me, looking confused. Muckle wiggled, barking at some of the other dogs going past on their way out.

I took a deep breath. "The private lesson thing? I don't want to wait," I blurted out. "I mean, I was wondering—is it only for agility, or other stuff too? Because Muckle's still having trouble with housebreaking, and I was hoping maybe you could come by tomorrow and, you know—"

Okay, this wasn't coming out nearly as smoothly or flirtatiously as I'd imagined it. And I was so sure Robert wouldn't approve of my technique. I could feel my face going bright red.

"Oh!" Adam smiled. "Sure, that sounds fine. I have a training class that ends at three—I could swing by your place afterward. How's that?"

"Perfect!" I blurted out. "I mean, that sounds good." I quickly told him where I lived. Muckle squeaked and wiggled harder, and I realized I was squeezing him too tightly. Releasing my grip, I forced myself to smile at Adam like a normal person. "See you tomorrow."

Chapter ● Thirteen
Flirt-line Sunday

By lunchtime on Sunday, I was a nervous wreck. As I sat in the kitchen trying to choke down some food, the back door swung open. I jumped, my heart fluttering with panic. But I relaxed when Robert walked in.

"Oh, thank goodness," I told him as Muckle started jumping around in his usual greeting ritual. "I thought you were one of my parents!"

Ignoring the puppy, Robert helped himself to one of my carrot sticks and sat down across from me. "Where are they? I thought you said they wouldn't be home today." He popped the carrot into his mouth. "It's going to be kind of embarrassing if they're hanging around, watching you make out with Adam."

"Shut up. There's not going to be any making out. Probably."

I blushed. "Anyway, Mom's at some charity luncheon that will probably last until dinnertime, and Dad's playing golf."

"Good. This is so exciting!" Robert clasped his hands in front of him like someone's old granny. "My little girl, getting ready for her first date!"

"Not really," I argued. "I went to the seventh-grade dance with Ben Reeves. He even got me a corsage."

"Doesn't count." Robert leaned his elbows on the table and surveyed my T-shirt, stretched-out old sweatpants, and flip-flops. "You're not planning to wear that, are you?"

"Of course not." I got up and dumped my plate and glass in the sink. "I was waiting for my fashion consultant to arrive."

He grinned. "At your service. Now, are we going for a sexy-sultry look, or more of a sweet innocent girly-girl look?"

"Neither." I shook my head. "This is supposed to be a dog training session, remember? I need to look normal and be able to walk and stuff. No tight skirts. No platform heels."

Robert frowned, then shrugged. "Fine. I can work with sporty and comfortable. Come on, let's go get started."

Soon we were digging through my closet. Thanks to Robert's frequent shopping sprees, it was overstuffed with options—most of them totally inappropriate for this particular occasion. Robert briefly tried to talk me into a way-too-short-and-slinky sweater dress before giving up and picking out my cutest jeans and a greenish-blue top that brought out the color of my eyes.

"You look gorgeous," he declared as I studied myself in the full-length mirror on the back of my door. "Casual yet chic. Adam will love it."

"Thanks." I glanced at Muckle, who had knocked over my wastebasket and was chasing all the bits of paper and used Kleenex under my bed. "I should probably take the Muckster for a walk before Adam gets here." I shivered as I said it. Adam was coming here! To my house, to see me! Well, technically he was coming to see Muckle. But also me.

"No time for dog walking," Robert said sternly. "We still have to do your hair and makeup."

I hesitated, looking at Muckle and then at my own reflection. I'd taken the puppy out for a quick piddle before I ate, but we hadn't gone on a real walk yet that day, let alone worked on our training.

Still, wasn't that what Adam was coming to help me with? Maybe it would be better if Muckle was a little hyper. That might make this whole situation seem more legit. You know, just in case Adam hadn't caught on to the subtext yet.

"Fine. But let's not go crazy with the makeup, okay?" I told Robert. "No glitter shadow. No hot-pink lipstick. Actually, make that no lipstick at all—gloss only." I too could sound stern.

Robert looked disappointed, but he nodded. "Soft and subtle and fresh. Got it."

He went to work. When I was looking as fresh and pulled together as possible, Robert turned his attention to Muckle.

"The mutt is looking a little shabby next to his gorgeous

owner," he said. "Shouldn't you, like, brush him or something?"

"Good idea." I collected a couple of Muck's grooming tools and tossed one to Robert. "You take the back half, I'll do the front."

Robert caught the brush and stared at it. "You want me to brush him?"

I grabbed Muckle and sat him on the bed, plopping down cross-legged next to him. "You're good with people hair," I said as I started combing out Muckle's thick ruff. "Puppy fur isn't that much different."

Robert hesitated, then shrugged and sat down on Muckle's other side. Soon we were both working on the puppy's silky coat. Muckle wiggled around and tried to bite my comb a couple of times, but mostly he seemed to enjoy the grooming session. I was surprised to notice that after his initial reaction, Robert actually seemed to be enjoying it too. Come to think of it, this was probably the first time I'd ever caught him having a good time while interacting with my puppy. If Muckle could win him over, maybe there was hope for my family yet!

When Muckle was looking coiffed and gorgeous, Robert checked his vintage robot-print Swatch. "Okay, you're both looking snazzy, and Adam should be here in, like, fifteen minutes. I'd better jet."

"Do you have to?" I'd gotten so caught up in our primping that I'd almost forgotten why we were doing it. Suddenly all my nerves were back.

He was already heading for the door. "Call me the second

the date is over," he called back over his shoulder. "I want all the juicy deets!"

"Promise." I followed him downstairs. Muckle came too, his newly smooth and shiny fur swishing around his legs.

Once Robert was gone, I paced around the empty house, getting more nervous by the second. "What do you think, Muck?" I asked the puppy, who was bouncing along beside me. "Are we ready for this?"

He let out an excited bark. As usual, he was ready for anything. Me? I wasn't so sure. But there was no turning back now.

Fifteen minutes passed. Then another five. Adam was late.

What if he didn't show? I hadn't really considered the possibility until that moment. I went and stared out the front window. Nothing.

Noticing that Muckle had disappeared, I hurried to find him. He was in the living room chewing on a gold-tasseled throw pillow. Oops.

"No! Bad puppy." I pulled the pillow away from him and examined it. There were a few tiny teeth marks along the edge, but nothing too—

BZZZ!

The doorbell startled me, making me jump and drop the pillow. Muckle pounced on it, growling playfully.

"Stop that." I grabbed him, kicking the pillow under the sofa to deal with later. Then I hurried to the front door.

When I swung it open, Adam was standing there. He smiled at me and Muckle. A battered backpack was slung over one shoulder, making him look like a superhot hobo.

"Hi. Sorry I'm late," he said. "One of the dogs in my last class had a meltdown at the weave poles, and we had to work through it and end on a good note."

"Oh. No biggie. We were just hanging out." I set Muckle down.

The puppy barked and leaped up on Adam's legs. A second later he backed away, squatted down—and peed on the polished parquet floor!

"Muckle! No!" I cried, face flaming. I grabbed the puppy and rushed him outside, but it was too late. There was a yellow puddle right inside the door. Good thing the rug that went there was already out being dry-cleaned. Which was also thanks to Muckle, come to think of it.

"No worries, Lauren." Adam didn't seem fazed at all. "A lot of dogs urinate when they get excited, especially when they're young. Yelling at them won't solve the problem—it can actually make it worse. But don't worry, it usually goes away as the pup gets older and more confirmed in his housebreaking."

From there, he launched into a whole spiel about various housebreaking methods and what I should be doing to help Muckle learn that the house was not a toilet. I listened while I cleaned up the puddle.

Okay, so far this wasn't exactly how I'd pictured this day going. But never mind. I had asked for help with housebreaking, after all. And it was pretty obvious that Muckle needed all the help he could get.

Once the floor was clean, Adam suggested taking Muckle out into the backyard. "Okay," I said. "But I should warn you, the yard isn't fenced or anything. It's against the rules of the homeowners' association."

Adam frowned, but then nodded. "No problem," he said. "We'll make do."

We went out there, and Adam pulled a superlong leash out of his backpack and switched it out with Muckle's regular leash. He started talking about using a long leash to teach Muckle to come, and also went into more housebreaking stuff. I was trying to listen and look cute at the same time, which wasn't easy, since Adam was following Muckle around the yard, letting him run as much as he wanted. Within minutes I was out of breath.

Then Adam switched the leash back to Muck's regular one and handed it to me, and we went through some of our usual exercises. Once or twice he grabbed me by the arm to correct my grip or something, which sent that electric spark through me just like the first time we'd touched. Was he feeling it too?

"Good," he said as Muckle and I performed a nearly perfect heel and turn after several not-so-great attempts.

"Thanks." I glanced at him. His blue eyes were so intense they almost burned. My mouth went dry as our eyes locked for a moment. Then Muckle barked at a bird flying past, and Adam glanced at him.

"Okay," he said. "Let's move on. . . ."

Finally, as we were working on some more leash exercises,

Muckle stopped and lifted his leg on Dad's favorite rosebush. As soon as he'd finished his business, Adam hurried over with a liver snap he'd pulled out of his pocket.

"Good boy!" he cried. "What a good pup!"

Muckle went crazy with joy, gobbling up the treat and then leaping around like a loon. I smiled as I watched Adam jump around with him. The guy really did have the magic touch with dogs.

He caught me watching and grinned sheepishly. "Sorry," he said, running a hand through his dark hair. "My mum says I'm at least half dog myself sometimes, or so it seems."

"That's okay. It's cool, actually. I wish I had that kind of rapport with dogs. I feel like I'm way behind since I never got to have one before."

He reached over and touched me on the arm, sending off another little firework display on my skin. "Don't fret, you're doing just fine," he said. "In fact, I'd say you're one of my best puppy K students right now."

"Well, you're definitely my favorite puppy K teacher," I countered daringly, channeling one of the sassy heroines from Robert's romance films.

He chuckled. "Thanks. Should we head in? I think we finally wore Muckle out. He could probably use a drink and a rest. He won't learn much when he's too tired to focus."

I glanced at the puppy. He'd stopped jumping around as soon as Adam had. Now he was flopped on the ground at my feet, watching Adam.

"Yeah, come on in," I said.

We went back inside. Muckle perked up as soon as he slurped up some water from his bowl, so we went out to the living room, and Adam showed me and Muckle more training stuff. When Muckle spotted the throw pillow under the sofa, we even learned a "drop it" command. Okay, so Muckle only dropped it about 50 percent of the time. Still, that was 50 percent more often than before.

Finally, when the puppy started yawning, Adam checked his watch. "That may be all his brain can handle for one day," he said with a smile.

"Yeah." I felt a moment of panic. He couldn't leave yet! Not when I was just starting to feel like we were really connecting! "Uh, do you want something to drink? There's soda, or juice. . . ."

He glanced at his watch again. "Sure, thanks, that'd be great."

I was very aware of him following me into the kitchen. Waving him toward a chair, I bustled around pouring us each some soda. Adam watched me, ruffling Muckle's ears as the puppy rubbed against his legs.

"You've got a sweet pup here, Lauren," Adam said as I set his glass in front of him. "He's got a super temperament and tons of potential."

That was pretty much what he'd said at the dog park, but I didn't mind the repetition. "Thanks," I said, sitting down across from him. "I wish I could convince my parents of that."

"What do you mean?" He kept rubbing Muckle's ears while the puppy panted with joy.

I sipped my soda. "Let's just say they weren't crazy about the idea of getting a dog."

With that, I found myself telling him the whole story. Adam listened quietly, actually looking interested.

"Wow," he said when I'd finished. "I don't know how I'd survive without a dog or two around. But now I'm extra glad you found my class. If you keep working at it, Muckle will turn into a dog even your parents can love. Even if it means more private lessons or whatever."

"Thanks." I smiled at him. He smiled back. There was a moment of silence, and we both sipped our drinks at the same time.

"So," Adam said after another moment. "Are you having fun in class so far?"

"Definitely! It's great." Realizing I might have sounded a little too enthusiastic, I added, "We're all having fun. Um, I mean I know Rachel and Jamal are too—Rachel even took your class a second time, after all."

He was nodding. "That vizsla of hers is a handful. I hope she sticks it out with her, though. They'd probably do well in agility, too—it would be a good outlet for all that energy."

"Yeah."

Another moment of silence. It was so quiet I could hear soft snuffling from under the table. Muckle had fallen asleep.

I scanned my mind for something to talk about. Maybe I should ask him about himself. Everyone liked talking about themselves, right?

Besides, I really did want to know more about Adam. I wanted to know everything about him. His favorite color, his taste in music, his hopes and fears and dreams. But I figured I'd start with the easy stuff.

"Speaking of agility," I said, breaking the silence, "how'd you first get into it?"

He brightened. "Oh, I've been competing since I was a young lad," he said. "See, my family had this whip-smart collie that was always getting into mischief. When she got bored and ate a hole in the wall one day, my parents threatened to get rid of her."

I grimaced. "Sounds kind of like me and Muckle."

"Yeah. Anyway, I was determined to keep her, so I started looking for ways to keep her occupied. A lad at the vet's office told me about an agility class he knew of, and that was all she wrote." He smiled, his blue eyes far away and nostalgic. "That dog was a natural—she ended up being my first champion. First of many."

Coming from anyone else, that might have sounded like bragging. But he sounded sweet and humble—as if he was giving all the credit to the dogs instead of himself.

He went on to share a few more highlights of the doggy adventures of his youth. After that, we talked about his plans for the future.

"After graduation, I want to open up my own dog-training business full-time," he said. "Make it my life's work, you know?"

"Awesome. You'll be great at that," I told him.

"Hope so. My parents, they'd like to see me go to college." He swished his ice cubes around in his drink. "But I'd rather take a few business classes part-time while I get started, you know? Why put off what I want to do just because they don't think it's the proper way?"

I nodded sympathetically. "My parents are the same. They never listen to what I think about anything, pretty much. My sister, on the other hand . . ."

"Like how they didn't want you to get a dog." He smiled ruefully. "I suppose they're all the same. In any case, I'm not going to give up my plans for anyone, even them."

"Good for you." I smiled. "So what else do you like to do besides the dog thing? Are you into music or movies or anything?"

"Oh, you know," he said vaguely. "I'll catch a film now and then when I have time."

"What's your favorite genre?" I asked. "Mystery, action, horror . . . ?"

He took another sip of soda. "I don't really mind. Whichever." Just then Muckle's tags jingled under the table. Adam peered down and smiled. "Look, he's dreaming. I love when they do that—act like they're running when they're sound asleep."

Glancing down, I saw Muckle's legs jerking around. His eyes were shut tight.

"Yeah, it's pretty cute," I agreed. "He does that a lot. My dad says he's too hyper even when he's asleep."

Adam laughed. "That reminds me of this training client I had once who swore his dog had a sleep disorder. . . ."

With that, he was off and running again, describing yet another dog from his past. It was interesting, though I was starting to wonder if he ever talked about anything but dogs. For instance, he hadn't asked me much about myself. Well, except for the dog-related parts, of course.

But was that so bad? I'd wanted someone with a passion, after all. And Adam definitely had that.

Besides, this was just one more thing that made him different. Most guys weren't that good at talking about anything except themselves. At least that was how it had always seemed to me, based on every guy I'd ever met. Especially Robert. He'd probably never stop talking about himself if I didn't smack him upside the head now and then.

As he finished his story about the sleep-deprived dog, Adam gulped down the rest of his soda, then checked his watch. "Listen, I've really got to go now," he said, standing. "But it's been great hanging out with you, Lauren. I wish I could stay longer."

"Yeah." I jumped to my feet. "Me too."

Muckle woke up and came out to see what was going on. His tail wagged, and he barked at Adam.

"See you in class, little fella." Adam gave him a pat. "Try not to pee on your mum's shoes before then, eh?"

I laughed. "I'll walk you out."

We headed for the front door with Muckle tagging along. When we got there, Adam stopped and turned to face me.

"Well . . ." he said, then paused.

I held my breath. He was gazing at me with a meaningful look on his face. What was he thinking? Did he want to ask me out? Or maybe . . . could he be thinking about kissing me?

My heart pounded at the thought. I hoped the Listerine I'd swished around my mouth earlier was still holding. Was I supposed to close my eyes when he leaned in, or wait until his lips actually touched mine? This would be my first kiss, and I wanted to make sure I did it right. Especially since it was happening with the man of my dreams . . .

Adam cleared his throat, looking uncomfortable. Aw! Was he feeling as nervous about this as I was? It was a strange thought, but a sweet one. I knew what Robert would say: *Go for it! Don't wait for him to kiss you—just kiss him yourself!*

But I wouldn't dare. Would I?

"So," Adam said, interrupting my frantic interior monologue. "Um, it'll be twenty-five dollars for today's session."

I stared at his lips, my body swaying toward his a little more as if pulled by a magnetic force. Then I blinked. Wait, what?

"Um . . ." My face grew hot as I took in what he'd just said.

He wasn't staring at me because he was thinking about kissing me. He was wondering if I was going to pay him for the training!

This was a disaster. Well, a near disaster. At least I hadn't actually gone ahead and tried to kiss him. That would have been a disaster. On an epic scale. As in, Vesuvius-level epic. What would he have thought? Talk about humiliating!

"Okay, yeah, sorry," I said quickly. "Er, just let me grab some cash. Be right back."

I rushed off, hoping he hadn't noticed that my face was now

lobster red. How could I have been so stupid? This hadn't been a date to him at all. It had been a job! Just another dog-training client with a puppy that liked to piddle on the rug.

Then I realized I had another problem. I was broke. I'd spent the last of my cash at PetzBiz yesterday, buying more dog treats. How was I going to pay Adam? I couldn't exactly go back out there and tell him I'd thought today's training would be free, what with my massive crush on him and all that I'd somehow, stupidly, thought might be mutual. . . .

I thought about calling Robert, begging him to rush over with some money. But no, that would take too long. Besides, I'd just remembered my mom's petty cash drawer in the kitchen. She always kept a few bills there in case of emergency. Blowing out a sigh of relief, I yanked the drawer open and counted out what I needed. I'd just have to borrow it from Robert and replace it before Mom noticed.

Hurrying back out to the hall, I handed over the money. "Well, thanks for coming," I said in what I hoped was a businesslike tone.

"Anytime." He pocketed the cash. If he noticed I was acting weird, he didn't let on. "Thanks, Lauren. See you in class on Tuesday, eh?"

"See you then!" I maintained my perky smile until the front door shut behind him. Then I collapsed against it and pulled my phone out of my pocket to call Robert.

Chapter ● Fourteen
Tuesday

Robert was wearing a tweedy wool cardigan with leather elbow patches when he arrived to pick me up on Tuesday morning. So he was in a college-professor kind of mood today, apparently.

"Hurry up," he said as I climbed into the Volvo. "I still need to finish my French vocab sheet before first period."

"Where'd you disappear to yesterday after you dropped me off?" I clicked on my seat belt as he backed out of the driveway. "I texted you after Muckle's walk to see if you wanted to hang out, but you never texted back."

"Sorry. I was running an errand. Guess I missed the text." He reached over and switched off the CD player, which had been playing one of my favorite Skerrabra songs.

"Hey, I was listening to that," I protested.

"You know, Corc's accent is starting to get on my nerves a little," he said. "In fact, I'm starting to think the entire British Isles are way overrated."

I stared at him, perplexed. It was too early in the morning for such an abrupt change of subject.

"Huh?" I said. "Since when?"

He shrugged. "Since right now. I'm thinking it's time to try something new. Get over the angsty Anglo thing. Maybe this afternoon we should disguise ourselves as salsa dancers or something—you know, try to pick up some hot Latino guys."

I blinked, still not quite following his train of thought. "I can't do anything this afternoon," I reminded him. "Puppy class, remember?" My stomach flip-flopped as I said it.

"Oh, that." Robert shot me a sidelong look. "Actually, I've been meaning to talk to you about that."

"About what? About how puppies are too much trouble?" I rolled my eyes. "I've heard it before."

"No, not that. It's about Adam." He clutched the steering wheel tighter as he turned onto Main Street. "I know I said Adam was hot before, but I'm kind of over him now. I think you're too good for a guy like that."

I stared at him. "Is this about Sunday? Because I told you, I'm sure that's all my fault. Like you said, I should've just asked him out instead of hiding behind the whole training thing."

"It wasn't your fault," he insisted. "Any other guy would've picked up what you were laying down. Adam's just clueless, and that's a bad sign. I mean, if he couldn't see the opportunity he had with you, he's too stupid to be with you. Possibly too stupid to live." He frowned. "It sort of makes me think he's actually a huge jerk underneath that hunky exterior, you know?"

Okay, now he was starting to annoy me. Yes, we'd spent at least a billion hours dissecting what I'd done wrong on Sunday afternoon. And yes, Robert had been supportive and sympathetic as usual. But as of when we'd last discussed it the previous day at lunch, he'd still been all about the try, try again thing. So where had this bad attitude about Adam come from all of a sudden?

"Are you kidding me with this?" I demanded.

"I'm dead serious." He swung the car into an empty spot near the flagpole. "You snooze you lose, buddy. Sayonara. *Hasta la vista.* All that jazz."

I frowned. "That's not how it works. He's just really focused on dogs." I hesitated. "Right?"

Just then a beefy guy in a letterman jacket knocked on the window, wanting to talk to Robert about the French homework. So that was the end of the conversation.

I was glad about that. Whatever had suddenly gotten into Robert, I hoped it went away just as suddenly. Because I would need his help to figure out what to do about Adam. Puppy class was that afternoon, and I wasn't sure I was ready to face him again.

By the time the final bell rang at the end of the day, I'd worked myself up into a tizzy of nerves. "Oh, man," I moaned as Robert and I headed out to the parking lot. "I'm not sure I'm ready for this. Maybe I should skip class today."

"Maybe you should," Robert said immediately. "We could go shopping instead. Maybe catch a movie. You've been so tense lately—you could use a little fun, right?"

I sighed. So much for counting on him to help psych me up to face Adam. After that morning's conversation, I probably shouldn't have been surprised.

"No, forget it," I said, yanking open the car door. "I can't let Muckle down. Not when he's finally starting to learn some stuff."

Robert climbed into the driver's seat and glanced over at me. "But are you sure he's learning enough?" he countered. "I mean, face it—you're probably a little distracted by the teacher."

"More than a little," I agreed with a grimace.

He nodded sagely. "So maybe you're letting Muckle down by staying with Adam. Maybe what you really need is to find a different trainer. Preferably one who's old and fat and has hair growing out of his ears." He smirked. "Or better yet, her ears."

I didn't answer as he started the car. Could he have a point? Was my crush on Adam the reason Muckle wasn't doing better? The thought made me uneasy.

"So if you might ditch class anyway, can we stop for ice cream?" Robert asked as he pulled out of the parking lot. "I'm craving a chocolate infusion."

I hesitated, thinking about Adam and Muckle and then back to Adam again. Specifically, the way he'd looked at me while waiting for his money. Not to mention the way I'd looked at him. Could he possibly have guessed what I was thinking? Ugh. If so, I'd never be able to show my face in PetzBiz again.

"I guess," I mumbled at last.

We were still working on our cones when we got to my house. "Hang on," Robert said, licking his fingers as we walked toward the front door. "Let me finish out here so your mom doesn't freak out about drips on her rugs."

"Good plan." I crunched the edge of my cone, but I barely tasted it or the peppermint swirl ice cream inside. Was I doing the right thing by skipping puppy class? I tried to tell myself it was no big deal. I could always go back on Saturday. I just needed a little time to figure things out, that was all. . . .

"Lauren!" My mother's sharp voice broke me out of my thoughts. "Why are you standing out in the yard? Get in here and deal with your dog—he just chewed up another pair of my sunglasses!"

Uh-oh. "Sorry, Mom." I tossed the last bit of my cone into the bushes and hurried inside, wiping my hands on my jeans.

Muckle looked completely unrepentant. He danced around, obviously thrilled to see me, as always.

Mom had followed me in, though Robert was still outside. "He also messed on the laundry room floor this morning," Mom informed me. "I suppose I should be glad it wasn't the rug again, but still. This has got to stop, Lauren. Or else we—"

"It will," I interrupted hastily, not wanting to give her the chance to finish that sentence. "I swear. The dog trainer says he's making progress." Grabbing Muckle, I hurried toward the door. "And we have another class today, remember? Which reminds me, we'd better go. Later, Mom!"

Robert looked surprised when I emerged and shoved him toward the Volvo. "What?" he mumbled through a half-chewed mouthful of cone.

"Hurry. We're going to be late as it is." I tossed Muckle into the passenger seat, then climbed in myself.

Robert opened the driver's-side door and peered in. "Hold on. I thought we weren't doing puppy class today."

"I changed my mind." I yanked down my seat belt and snapped it on. "There's no time to look for a different trainer. It's Adam or nothing."

A shiver ran through me as I said it, and I realized I'd been lying to myself. I didn't want to drop that class. And not just because my family was on my case about Muckle. Okay, maybe that was a big part of it. But it wasn't the only part. I knew I couldn't run away from this. I'd been fixated on Adam from the moment I first saw him. I had to figure out what that meant, and what I was supposed to do about it.

When Muckle and I reached the training ring, class had already started. Jamal spotted me coming and waved.

"There she is," he said.

Adam turned and saw me too. "Lauren!" he exclaimed with a smile. "We were wondering what happened to you."

"Sorry I'm late," I said as Muckle leaped toward Adam in his usual boisterous greeting. I felt breathless, and not only because we'd sprinted in from the parking lot. Adam's smile always dazzled me, especially when it was aimed in my direction. Had he really missed me when I hadn't showed up? Was he starting to realize I could be more than just another student? I wasn't sure, but the possibility was tantalizing, and suddenly I was very glad I'd changed my mind about ditching.

"No worries, you haven't missed much yet—we just got going." Adam patted Muckle, then gestured for us to take a spot with the group. "We were about to start with a review of what we did last time. Let's just—"

He cut himself off as the Chihuahua suddenly barked and flung itself on top of the pug, who flopped over and lay there, rolling its bulging eyes helplessly. "Ack!" the pug's owner cried. "Get it off!"

"What should I do?" the Chihuahua's owner exclaimed.

Adam hurried over to break up the fight and talk down the owners. While he was busy doing that, I stepped over to join Jamal and Rachel, who were standing together on the other side of the ring.

"Glad you made it, Lauren," Jamal said. "We thought you'd gotten tired of us."

His smile wasn't as dazzling as Adam's, but it was so friendly that I couldn't help returning it. "Nope, just running late today," I said. "So how are you guys? Do anything fun over the weekend?"

"Not me," Rachel said. "I had this big history paper due

yesterday, so I mostly—Gizi! Quit that!"

The vizsla puppy had just noticed that the brown-and-white mixed breed's owner, a geeky-looking fourteen-year-old guy, had a loose shoelace. She pounced on it, and Rachel stepped over to help the guy detach himself, while the mixed-breed pup jumped around, barking and getting in the way.

I was watching the action when Jamal leaned closer, nudging me with his shoulder. "So I caught a movie over the weekend," he said. "The theater had a poster up for that new zombie flick. You heard about it?"

"Sure!" My eyes lit up. "It looks excellent."

"Yeah." He grinned. "So it opens this coming weekend, and I was thinking—hey!" Jamal yelped in surprise as Muckle suddenly noticed what was going on with Gizi and the other dog and raced over to join in. Unfortunately, the most direct route involved him darting right between Jamal's legs.

"Muckle!" I cried as he yanked me forward. It was amazing the amount of g-force a small puppy could exert. I felt the leash slip out of my hand, but not before I also felt my body collide with Jamal's.

"Whoa!" he exclaimed, catching me by the shoulders. "You okay?"

I looked up at him. His face was very close as he looked back, his expression serious for once.

"Um, I'm fine," I said, backing away.

At least that was what I meant to do. Except that by now, Ozzy was dashing back and forth, trying to join in the play session going on nearby, and I tripped over him.

"Oof!" I grunted as I plowed into Jamal's chest. Again.

He laughed softly as he staggered backward, almost crashing into the barrier around the ring. "We have to stop meeting this way," he quipped.

I noticed that this time we'd somehow ended up with one of his arms wrapped around my waist. And he didn't seem to be in a hurry to release me.

"I'm really sorry," I mumbled, my face flaming.

His arm squeezed gently. I suddenly became aware that his other hand was resting on my upper arm. For one giddy moment, it felt as if we were slow dancing.

Then Adam hurried toward us. "Everything okay over here?" he asked, his blue eyes flicking from the tangle of puppies over by Rachel to the tangle of, well, me and Jamal. Was it my imagination, or did he look startled—and maybe a little perturbed?

"No. I mean yes." I shoved back from Jamal, who immediately let go of me and stepped back as well. "I mean, we're fine. The puppies—the leashes—we just—"

"Lauren tripped and fell on me," Jamal told the instructor with a smile. "But I think I'll survive."

Adam nodded and stepped over to help disentangle the puppies. He grabbed Muckle's leash and led him over to me.

"Here you go, Lauren," he said without quite meeting my eye. "And listen—do you have a moment after class? I want to talk to you about something."

"S-sure," I stammered, suddenly going so numb I could barely hang on to the leash. "No problem."

"Good." He nodded, then stepped into the center of the ring to resume class.

I barely heard a word he said for the rest of the hour. Muckle really must have been learning something, because somehow we managed to get through the class without embarrassing ourselves again, even though I wasn't particularly effective as a handler. I was vaguely aware of Jamal and Rachel speaking to me now and then, but I couldn't do much more than nod in response.

Finally class was over. Every thought in my mind had coalesced into one giant question, pulsing like a neon sign—what did Adam want to talk to me about?

You know those movies where someone has an angel on one shoulder and a devil on the other, telling him opposite things? Well, I had that. Only it wasn't an angel and a devil talking to me. It was happy, optimistic Muckle on one shoulder, yapping that Adam had come to his senses and realized I was the girl of his dreams, and that after class he was planning to ask me to run away to Ireland with him to live happily ever after.

On the other shoulder was my sister Britt, who'd always been a pessimist. Or a realist, as she called it. She kept sniping that I'd been an idiot on Sunday, that Adam had figured out what I was up to and wanted to tell me I was such a blithering moron that he wasn't going to let me take his class anymore.

The girl with the hound buttonholed Adam on her way out of the ring, babbling at him about whatever problems she and her puppy were having. After that, the pug girl hurried over to thank him for saving her pup from the scary Chihuahua.

As I was waiting, Jamal and Rachel came over. "Walk you out?" Jamal asked in his affable way.

I shot a look at Adam. "Um, Adam wanted to talk to me," I reminded him. Hadn't he heard? He'd been standing right there. "I'd better see what he wants. You guys don't have to wait."

"Oh. Okay." Jamal hesitated, but finally tossed me one more smile and then headed out after Rachel.

It seemed to take forever for the other students to finish yapping at Adam. But finally the last of them disappeared, and we were alone.

He walked over to me. "Thanks for waiting," he said to Muckle. Well, okay, he was probably talking to me. But his gaze was trained on Muckle, who was lying stretched out on the cool tile floor at my feet.

"Sure," I said, trying for an easy, casual tone and probably failing miserably. "What's up?"

He wet his lips, then glanced at the ceiling. "It's no big deal," he mumbled, sounding uncharacteristically uncertain. "It's just, the training session on Sunday was fun, but I—that is, when I saw your friend Robert yesterday—I mean, I guess I just . . ."

I stared at him. What in the world was he talking about? When and where had he seen Robert—and why in the world hadn't Robert told me?

Adam's next words made me forget all that. "So I was wondering if you'd like to, you know, go out sometime?" His eyes finally flicked down to meet mine. "Like, on a date?"

"Really?" I blurted out. Yeah, I know—not exactly the coolest of responses. But I couldn't help it.

He nodded. "There's this big agility competition over in East Carrelton on Saturday afternoon—I was going to head over there right after class with my dogs," he said, his words coming out so fast I could hardly take them in. "I was thinking maybe you'd want to come cheer us on? You know—since you're interested in agility anyway. I mean, it would be cool to have someone there. It can be tough to juggle both dogs sometimes, and well, I could use—anyway, then maybe we could grab something to eat afterward or something."

His gaze had wandered ceilingward again while he was talking, but now he shot me an uncertain look. I couldn't believe it. Was he actually nervous about asking me out? That was so unexpected—and so sweet—that I almost laughed out loud.

"Yeah," I said instead. "I mean sure, that sounds like fun. I'd love to."

"Great, great." He looked relieved. "Okay, then. I guess I'll see you Saturday?"

I shivered. "I'll see you Saturday."

Chapter ● Fifteen
A weird week

Robert was examining a package of goldfish flakes in the aquarium aisle when I almost bowled him over with a big, surprise hug. "You'll never believe what just happened!" I cried as Muckle leaped around our legs, barking happily.

Yanking his right arm free of my grip, Robert tossed the fish food back on the shelf. "You won the lottery? Cool. Then you can pay me back for these puppy classes."

"Very funny." I let go of him and stepped back. "Actually, this is way better than the lottery. Adam just asked me out!"

I grinned, waiting for him to freak out. Actually, I was sort of wishing I'd made him go outside before telling him. What if Adam heard his whoops of triumph?

But no—this news couldn't wait. Anyway, Robert wasn't

whooping. He wasn't making any noise at all, actually. A frown crept across his face as he stared at me.

"Oh," he said after a moment. "Yeah, I thought that might happen."

I blinked. "You don't seem very happy about it." Suddenly I remembered that Adam had mentioned Robert's name, and I belatedly put two and two together. "Wait—you didn't, like, tell him to ask me, did you? Is that what he was talking about? Oh man, you did, didn't you?"

Robert held up his hands. "Down, girl," he said. "I admit it, okay? That was my errand yesterday. I stopped over here after I dropped you off and hung around until after Adam was finished with his training class."

"So you did tell him to ask me out?" I cried. "Oh, man—talk about humiliating!" Suddenly an even worse thought occurred to me. "Wait—you didn't, like, pay him to do it, did you?"

"No! Of course not." He looked insulted. "I didn't even tell him to do it. All I did was explain what happened on Sunday. Let him know he missed his cue."

"Oh, man," I moaned again.

"No, listen." Robert grabbed my arm. "It's cool. He actually felt bad about the misunderstanding. I think he already thought you were cute."

"Really?" I was still humiliated. But now I was intrigued, too. "Okay, I wish you'd told me you were planning to talk to him." I paused, thinking about that. "Hold on—scratch that.

Never mind. If I'd known, I never would have let you do it."

His mouth twisted. "No kidding."

"Anyway, I guess the important thing is, it worked." I shivered as I remembered how sweet and shy Adam had been when he'd asked me out. "Thanks, pal."

"Anytime, buddy." Robert hesitated, twisting his leather elbow patch between his fingers. "But listen, after talking to Adam yesterday, I'm not sure about him."

I grabbed a plastic fish-tank plant out of Muckle's mouth. "What do you mean?"

"I mean, I'm not sure he's such a dream guy after all." Robert shrugged. "Yeah, the accent's cool, and there's no denying he's easy on the eyes. But I'm starting to think that's all he's got going."

"Huh?" I straightened up and frowned. "You're crazy. Adam's awesome. Even the dogs think so."

"That's the thing." Robert glanced down at Muckle, who was staring longingly at the fish plant I'd returned to the shelf. "The guy seems pretty hyper focused on the whole dog thing. Like, to the point he doesn't seem to have much interest in anything else."

"So he has a passion," I retorted. "I like that in a guy."

Robert still looked troubled. "But does he really have time for a relationship? Is he even interested in one? You're too good to play second fiddle to a bunch of mutts, Lauren."

I rolled my eyes. "Don't be melodramatic."

"No, I'm serious." Robert frowned at me. "It's not like you're some hopeless case who has to take the first guy who shows inter-est. Lots of guys think you're cute."

"That's news to me," I shot back. "Name one. And my dad doesn't count."

"What about Jamal?" Robert raised an eyebrow. "It's pretty blazing obvious he's got the hots for you."

"What?" I could feel my face going pink. "Jamal? He's cool, but we're just friends."

The eyebrow arched higher. "Does Jamal know that?"

"Shut up." I couldn't think of a better retort. Why was Robert talking about Jamal when Adam had just asked me out? "I thought you were supposed to be my best friend," I added irritably.

"I am your best friend."

"Then act like it. You should be happy for me right now, okay? Especially since you're the one who helped make it happen."

"Yeah." He was frowning again. "Yippee me."

Muckle was nosing at the fake kelp again, which seemed like our cue to get out of there. "Come on," I said. "I think Muckle's ready for a walk. Let's go."

"What do you think?" I held up a pair of cute patterned leggings. "These and a tunic top, maybe? Too casual, or just casual enough?"

Robert shrugged, barely looking up. He was sprawled on my bed, flipping through one of my mom's old-lady fashion mags.

I stuck the leggings back in the closet, then yanked Muckle away from my shoe rack. "Don't eat those," I told the puppy sternly.

"I haven't decided which ones to wear on Saturday yet." Shooting a look over my shoulder, I added, "And somebody isn't being much help."

That made Robert look up. "Oh, you wanted my advice?" he said tartly. "That's funny. I thought you were ignoring that this week."

I sighed. Things had been tense since our chat the previous afternoon. That was Robert for you—he was a talented sulker when the mood struck him. I was trying to be patient and ignore his attitude, but it was getting old. Why did he have to get in a snit now, when I really could have used his advice?

"Fine," I said. "Then maybe I'll just borrow Mom's favorite plaid slacks." I sneaked a peek over to gauge Robert's reaction. If that offense to fashion didn't snap him out of it, nothing would.

Just then my phone buzzed. Fishing it out of my pocket, I saw that the call was coming from a number I didn't recognize. I almost didn't answer, but then I wondered if it could be Adam.

"Hello?" I said.

"Lauren? Hi, it's Jamal."

I stiffened. "Jamal?" How had he found out my number? It was unlisted. "Um, hi. What's up?"

Out of the corner of my eye, I saw Robert sit up abruptly. He stared at me, his eyes glittering with interest.

"Not much," Jamal said. "Uh, except I was wondering—that is, if you're not doing anything on Saturday after class, I thought maybe we could check out that zombie movie."

I swallowed hard. Robert was leaning forward, as if trying to hear the other end of the conversation. I clutched the phone tightly.

"Oh," I said. "Um, that would be fun, except I can't. I already have plans for Saturday after class. Sorry."

"Oh, okay." Jamal sounded disappointed. "Maybe some other time, huh? See you in class."

"Yeah. See you." I hung up and glared at Robert. "How did Jamal get my number?" I demanded.

He frowned. "Why'd you say no? I know you're dying to see that stupid monster movie."

"It's a zombie movie. And so not the point," I snapped. "Seriously, did you tell Jamal to ask me out?"

"Absolutely not." He shrugged. "Okay, I might have encouraged him a little. But he was already thinking about it all on his own."

I crossed my arms over my chest, glaring at him. Sensing my growing fury, Muckle crouched down and whined.

"I can't believe this!" I cried. "You knew I was already going out with Adam on Saturday! All you did was force me to hurt Jamal's feelings. What if he's so hurt he doesn't even want to be friends anymore?"

"So again—why'd you say no?" Robert wasn't backing down. "Jamal's a much better prospect than Mr. Self-Absorbed Woof-Woof Man."

I gritted my teeth. "That's for me to decide! How dare you meddle in my love life?"

"If I didn't meddle, you wouldn't even have a love life," he countered. "Anyway, I'm just trying to fix my previous mistake. I never should have talked to Adam about you."

"So that's what this is about?" Suddenly I gasped as another thought popped into my mind. "Wait—so you decided Adam wasn't good enough for me after you had your little private chit-chat with him, huh? Is that what this is really about?"

He blinked. "What?"

"Maybe you liked what you saw even better face-to-face," I spat out. "Maybe you're trying to sabotage me so you can go for Adam yourself!"

"What? Are you serious? You can't—I wouldn't—why would I even—how could you—," he sputtered, his face going beet red. He jumped off the bed and stomped toward the door.

"Where are you going?" I demanded.

"Anywhere but here," he snapped back. The door slammed, and he was gone.

Chapter ✦ Sixteen
Friends

Robert and I still hadn't made up by the time school ended on Friday. Not only was I being forced to take the bus to and from school, but I'd also never felt more lonely. Oh, sure, I had a few other friends at County Day—girls who usually invited me to their parties, who I sat with at lunch whenever Robert was absent or in detention, and who I sometimes paired up with for projects and stuff.

But it wasn't the same. Robert and I argued all the time, of course. But our fights normally never lasted more than a day or so. We were just too close for that.

Or were we? The longer things went on, the more I wondered what would happen if we never made up. After all, Robert had ditched "BFFs" before, hadn't he? For the first time, I wondered what had become of all those anonymous blondes he'd mentioned when we'd first met.

I stared out the bus window all the way home on Friday afternoon, so worried that I barely even noticed the stale-corn-chips-and-feet smell of the bus. When I let myself into the house, Muckle was his usual hyper self. Miraculously, he hadn't chewed up or peed on anything that day—at least nothing Mom had noticed.

"What do you know—maybe there's hope for the little fur ball yet," she said, shooting Muckle the closest thing to a smile she'd ever given him as he leaped around, expressing his joy at my arrival. "Let's keep up the good work, Lauren, okay?"

"Will do, Mom." I kept a slightly worried eye on the gleeful puppy, remembering his reaction to Adam's arrival the other day. "Come on, Muckle," I said, grabbing him with one hand and his leash with the other. "Let's go out."

After he'd done his business, I was feeling restless. I was used to spending most of my free time with Robert, and without him I wasn't quite sure what to do with myself.

"Why don't I have any other friends, Muckle?" I muttered.

The puppy glanced up from sniffing a bug and let out a bark. I sighed.

"Of course you wouldn't understand," I told him, bending down to run my fingers through his furry ruff. "To a puppy, the whole world is a friend, right?"

I pulled out my phone and stared at it, tempted to call Robert and beg for forgiveness. Instead I got a better idea. Logging on to the Internet, I searched the name Rachel Kardos. The results popped up immediately.

"Great—she's listed," I told Muckle. Then I dialed Rachel's number.

She answered on the second ring. "Lauren?" she said when I identified myself. "Hi! What's up?"

"I was thinking about taking Muckle to the dog park in Springdale this afternoon," I said. "I was wondering if you and Gizi wanted to go?"

"Sure! That sounds fun," Rachel said. "I'm actually getting my hair cut in Springdale right now—I could meet you at the dog park in, like, half an hour if that's okay?"

"Cool. Let me see if my mom can give me a ride," I said. "If she can't, I'll have to take the bus, so I definitely won't make it in half an hour. But I'll text you back either way."

"Great. See you soon!" Rachel actually sounded happy that we had plans. Take that, Robert.

When I got back to the house, I found that I was in luck. Mom hadn't left yet for her weekly Friday charity meeting in Madison. She agreed to drop me and Muckle off at the dog park and pick us up an hour and a half later on her way back home.

Rachel was waiting by the gate when Muckle and I got out of the car. Gizi spotted us first and went crazy, barking and jumping around on the end of her leash. Muckle responded in the same way, and the two puppies enjoyed a happy reunion.

"Think they're glad to see each other?" Rachel asked with

a laugh, blowing a strand of blond hair out of her eyes as Gizi dragged her around.

"Hmm, hard to say," I joked. "Come on, let's go in."

This was Rachel's first visit to the dog park, so I gave her a quick tour. Once again, there were lots of dogs running around the main lawn, and others playing in the smaller pens or lapping water from the fountains. Even though it was only my second time there, I recognized a few of the dogs and their people—the stout older man with the boxer, the blond girl with the Brittany, a tattooed guy with a burly Rottweiler. Oops—and even the lady with the papillon was back, though luckily, she was wandering in the opposite direction and didn't see me and Muckle. A few other dogs looked kind of familiar too. Obviously Adam wasn't the only regular at the dog park.

"The agility courses are down here," I told Rachel as we reached the first of the agility pens.

Her eyes lit up with interest. "Adam keeps talking about agility, right? He thinks I should try it with Gizi."

I laughed. "I get the feeling Adam thinks every dog should try agility. He keeps telling me Muckle has natural talent."

"Yeah? That's cool." Rachel leaned on the fence and watched the dogs in the agility pen. A shepherd mix was practicing some jumps, barking joyfully every time it cleared one. Nearby, a young man was trying to convince a confused-looking Labrador retriever to go through the weave poles properly instead of just crashing through them.

I was half expecting to see Adam in there with his dogs too. But he was nowhere in sight.

"Come on," I told Rachel. "I think I see a free play pen. We can let the pups off leash in there."

Soon Muckle and Gizi were romping together in the pen. I'd brought a rubber ball, which they were mostly ignoring in favor of chewing on each other's ears and paws.

There was a wooden bench built into the fence line, and Rachel and I wandered over and sat down. "This place is really amazing," she said, glancing into the next pen, where an older couple was watching a pair of tiny lap dogs run around.

"I know, right?" I agreed. "It's like doggy nirvana."

"Yeah. I'm glad you called." Rachel smiled shyly at me. "I've been wanting to check this place out ever since Adam first mentioned it, but I didn't want to come alone."

Just then Gizi wiped out as she tried to chase Muckle around in a tight circle. I laughed as she sat up, looking surprised to find herself on the ground.

"Gizi's cool," I said. "I never even heard of a vizsla before I met you guys. How'd you end up with her?"

"Actually, it was my dad's idea." Rachel tugged on her hair, watching her puppy. "I wanted a dog, but I was thinking something smaller and a little, um, less active." Her gaze wandered briefly to the lap dogs next door. "But my dad decided if we were going to get a dog, it should be a good Hungarian dog." She rolled her eyes. "He's really into that stuff."

"Oh." I thought about telling her the real reason I'd chosen Muckle's breed, but I held back. I liked Rachel—I didn't want her to think I was a total ditz who based major life decisions on the nationality of her favorite rock stars.

"Anyway," Rachel went on, "I'm definitely thinking about trying the agility thing. Adam makes it sound like a lot of fun, and Gizi could definitely use more exercise."

"You could talk to Adam about some private lessons to start you off," I suggested, smiling as Gizi jumped right over Muckle, barking gleefully. "He has lots of clients like that. And he definitely knows his stuff—I ran into him here last week and saw his dogs. They're amazing."

"He does agility with them?" Rachel asked.

I nodded and shot her a sidelong look. "Actually, I'm going to watch Adam's dogs in a competition tomorrow after class," I admitted. "It's, you know, sort of, um, a date."

Rachel had been watching the puppies, but now her head swiveled quickly toward me. "A date? You mean—you and Adam?"

"Uh-huh." I ducked my head, suddenly feeling bashful. Was it too early in our friendship to share that type of thing? It had been so long since I'd hung out with a girl that I wasn't sure. "I guess we kind of bonded, and you know . . ."

"Oh, okay." Rachel smiled uncertainly. "I hope you guys have fun."

"Thanks." I hesitated. "Um, so you and Adam go to the same school, right? Does he—do you know if he dates a lot?"

Rachel's gaze had returned to the puppies. "I'm not sure," she said. "I don't really know him that well. I think he's had a few girl-friends, but nothing too serious." She stood up. "It looks like the puppies have run out some of their energy. Should we take them over to the agility place? I'd love to see how Gizi reacts. And I think I saw both those other dogs leaving, so it might be free now."

"Sure." I stood too. "Let's go."

We spent the next hour playing with the pups in the agility pen. Gizi took to the equipment just as quickly as Muckle had. Thanks to my private session with Adam, I was able to give Rachel a few tips about what to do. Before long, the vizsla was clearing the jumps and skittering across the dog walk like a pro.

Finally I checked my watch. "Oops, I should go," I said reluc-tantly. "My mom will be here to pick me up soon, and she'll prob-ably faint if she has to come into the dog park to look for me." I smiled ruefully. "Actually, she'll probably just leave without me and text me to take the bus."

Rachel laughed. "Not a dog person?"

"Not even close." I whistled and called Muckle. To my sur-prise, he actually stopped what he was doing—currently, sniffing around under the pause table—and ran over to me. "Good boy!" I told him as I snapped on his leash.

Rachel grabbed Gizi, and we headed out to the gate. "I'll wait with you until your mom gets here," Rachel offered. "My dad won't be back to get me for another twenty minutes anyway."

"Cool, thanks." I smiled at her, glad I'd decided to take a

chance and call her. I'd had a great time—and best of all, I'd barely thought about Robert or our fight for the past hour. Or stressed about my date with Adam the next day either.

"We should do this again soon," Rachel said, leaning against the fence. Both puppies flopped down at our feet, looking tired and content. "Maybe Jamal will come next time too. We should mention it to him tomorrow."

"Good idea." I kept my voice bright, but Jamal's name sent a pang of guilt through me. I knew how hard it was to ask someone out—after all, I'd just messed it up myself the previous week with Adam. Of course, it had been all Robert's fault that I'd had to turn Jamal down, but Jamal himself had been the one who'd paid the price.

Then again, maybe there was a way I could make it up to him. . . . I shot a sidelong, appraising glance toward Rachel. She was adorable and supersweet. Both she and Jamal were awesome people—down-to-earth, friendly, smart. Why not try to set them up? Who knew, maybe they'd end up double-dating with me and Adam sometime!

"Yeah, we should definitely mention it to Jamal," I went on brightly. "Although we won't be able to come here after class tomorrow, and not only because I have plans with Adam. I think Jamal was wanting to see that new zombie flick that opens this weekend."

"Zombies?" Rachel echoed. "I think I heard about that one."

"It's supposed to be awesome," I said. "Like I said, I think Jamal really wants to see it tomorrow. Opening weekend and all that, you know? But I don't think he's found anyone to see it with yet."

"Hmm." Rachel bent down to straighten Gizi's collar, making it impossible for me to read her expression.

Just then the blast of a car horn made me jump. Glancing over, I saw my mother's car idling at the curb. Muckle barked and leaped to his feet.

"There's my ride," I said. "I'd better go. See you tomorrow."

"See you tomorrow." Rachel waved as I hurried over to the curb.

"Who's that girl?" my mother asked as I climbed into the car with Muckle.

"Her name's Rachel. She goes to MVHS." I smiled. "She's a new friend."

It felt good to say that. I still missed Robert, but at least I wasn't sitting around like a pathetic loser, waiting for him to decide to start talking to me again. I was grateful to Rachel for making me feel like I had options, no matter how long it took Robert to come to his senses. And in return? Maybe I'd just done her—and Jamal, for that matter—a little favor in return.

Chapter ●Seventeen
Saturday

Puppy class seemed to last forever. And not in a good way. I fidgeted through Adam's talk about the value of socialization and rushed Muckle through the first few exercises. The giant countdown clock in my head just kept ticking down the seconds until my date with Adam—like a doomsday clock counting down the end of the world.

When Muckle and I returned to our seat after taking our turn demonstrating a sit-stay, Jamal gave me a thumbs-up. "The Muckster's really coming along," he whispered as I sat down beside him.

"You think so?" I glanced at my puppy, who was sitting alertly at my feet. Belatedly, I realized he'd been almost perfect all through class so far, even though I was more than a little distracted. "Yeah, I guess they're all learning, right?"

"Maybe not all." Jamal smirked and nodded toward the center

of the ring, where the lively retriever's owner was attempting vainly to convince her puppy to remain seated for more than a millisecond at a time.

I smiled weakly. Muckle's skills aside, I was glad that Jamal didn't seem to hold a grudge about being shot down. He truly was a great guy, which made me more determined than ever to make it up to him somehow. Preferably by hooking him up with Rachel. Had she taken my hint and talked to him about the zombie movie? I wasn't sure, but I didn't think so. Rachel had already been in the training ring when I'd arrived, and Jamal had rushed in just seconds before Adam called the class to order. Jamal and Rachel had said hi to each other, but they weren't exchanging any meaningful looks or anything as far as I could tell.

While Adam continued to work with the retriever and his owner, I leaned back in my seat, smoothing down my favorite print pants. I'd done my best to dress to impress that day. Without Robert there, I hadn't had to convince anyone that a miniskirt or evening gown weren't appropriate for a dog agility competition. That should have been a good thing, right? Weirdly, not so much. It just wasn't as much fun choosing an outfit without my personal fashion consultant. Besides that, Robert had a much better touch with makeup than I did. I could only hope my ham-fisted attempts at blush and eyeliner hadn't left me looking like a clown. Nobody was staring, so I figured it was probably okay.

After the retriever finally managed to perform an adequate sit-stay, it was Rachel's turn to give it a try. She headed to the center of the ring with Gizi. That meant it was time for step two of my plan.

"Rachel's mega cool, isn't she?" I whispered to Jamal. "She and I hung out at the dog park for a while yesterday. Actually, we were talking about that zombie movie—I think she wants to see it."

"For real?" Jamal shot a surprised look in Rachel's direction. "Funny. She doesn't strike me as the zombie type."

I shrugged. "You never know about people, right? Anyway, I never knew Rachel had such an amazing sense of humor. She's supercool, right?"

"Sure." Just then Ozzy noticed a Great Dane walking by outside the ring and tried to run over to say hi, which kept Jamal busy until Rachel returned to her seat. But I hoped I'd at least planted a seed in his head.

Another million years passed with all the urgency of frozen molasses. But finally, finally, finally Adam dismissed the class.

"Keep practicing, everyone," he called out. "I'll see you all next Tuesday."

It took another eon or two for the class to actually disperse. I was worried that Jamal might hang around wanting to chat or something, but I was pleased to notice that he and Rachel hurried off together after a quick good-bye to me. Two birds with one stone . . .

Finally the last of my classmates was gone, and Adam walked over to where I was sitting with Muckle on my lap. He looked a little nervous, though I had no idea whether that was because of the competition or our date. I knew which it was in my case, though. Even though I'd spent much of the past two weeks dreaming of this moment, now that it was here, my palms were clammy and my legs felt numb.

"Ready to go, then?" he asked, shifting his weight from one foot to the other. "I just need to swing by my house and pick up the girls."

"Sure." Thankfully my numb legs still seemed to work, and I followed him out of the store and over to his minivan. He opened the passenger-side door for me. I thought he was just being a gentleman until he started brushing at the seat.

"Sorry about the dog hair," he said. "Jinx likes to ride up front and direct traffic."

"It's okay." I forced a smile, telling myself I'd been smart to wear printed pants. Maybe they wouldn't show the hair as much. "I'm used to it. The Muckster isn't exactly bald, you know."

Adam chuckled and stepped back, and I hoisted Muckle and myself into the van. There was an odd smell in there, but I tried not to notice. Muckle sniffed around with interest, though.

"So this should be fun," Adam said as he started the van. "Shasta is first in her division right now, so the pressure's on. Lark's only a few points behind her, with two dogs in between."

"That's amazing," I said. "Congratulations!"

He shot me a surprised look. "Oh. Um, thanks. I'm actually hoping to move up with Lark soon. We should be able to beat the third-place dog today, no problem. The course designer for this

event always throws in a lot of tight twists and turns, and Fred—
that's the dog's name—tends to get moving so fast he gets ahead
of his handler on that kind of course."

"Hmm," I said, a little distracted by Muckle's wiggling. I tightened my grip just in time to stop him from leaping out of my arms
into Adam's lap.

Adam spun the wheel as he made the turn onto the highway.
"The bitch in second place is going to be tough, though—she's
super experienced, and her owner's taken a whole bunch of dogs
to the top."

It took a lot of self-control to stop myself from giggling at his
use of the word "bitch," even though I knew it was a totally legit
term for a female dog.

"Wow," I said, trying to sound mature and not at all giggly.
"You sure know a lot about the competition."

Once again, he looked slightly surprised. "Of course. That's
the only way to do well, right? Anyway, I've been working really
hard with Lark on the seesaw, which has always been her toughest
element. I think she's ready to surprise some people today."

We continued chatting about that day's competition as he
drove to his house. Well, mostly he continued chatting about it,
while I nodded a lot and did my best to hold on to Muckle, who
naturally would have preferred to go boinging around the van.

Adam lived in an older neighborhood of large brick homes
near MVHS. He left me in the van with the engine running while
he dashed inside, returning moments later with Shasta and Lark at

his heels. He opened the back door and the border collies jumped in. Muckle barked, the border collies barked back, and the whole van echoed like a giant tin can for a while. Adam didn't seem to notice as he jumped back in and pulled away from the curb.

"So Jinx isn't coming along today?" I asked, raising my voice above the barking.

"No, he's not reliable off leash," Adam replied. "I didn't want you to have to keep track of another dog while I'm competing."

"Oh." I couldn't help feeling a little sorry for the lively terrier.

Adam seemed to catch my tone. He glanced over at me. "Don't worry," he said with a smile. "Jinx will get his turn. We've got a flyball club meeting tonight."

"Flyball?" I'd heard him mention that before. From my Internet research, I knew it was a dog sport. But that was about all I knew.

He returned his gaze to the road. "It's a blast," he said. "Jinx is the height dog on our team—that's what we call the shortest dog, since it's how they decide the height of the jumps for the whole team, and . . ."

With that, he was off and running again. We spent the rest of the drive discussing all the intricacies of flyball. I hadn't known it had that many intricacies, actually. But it was interesting. Sort of.

Finally we pulled into the parking lot of Riverside High School, which was a couple of towns over from Maple View. "Is this where the competition is?" I asked.

"Yep." He pulled into an empty spot and cut the engine. "They set up the equipment on the playing fields."

As soon as we got out of the car, I could hear barking. Lots of barking. "I guess the playing fields are that way, huh?" I quipped.

"Right." Adam was busy clipping on his dogs' leashes. Both of them were alert and excited; Shasta stared intently in the direction of the barking, while Lark spun in circles and yipped.

Muckle had heard the barking too, of course. I kept a tight hold on his leash as he jumped around, barking and smelling things.

"Do you have a free hand?" Adam asked, leaning into the van. He came out holding an overstuffed tote bag, which he handed to me.

"Um, sure." Gripping Muckle's leash with my left hand, I slung the bag over my other shoulder. "Wow, it's heavy. What's in here?"

"Liver snaps, poo bags, water bottles—the usual." Adam slammed the door shut and glanced at me, his eyes flashing with excitement. "Let's go."

We hurried around the corner of the school to the sight of a three-ring circus. At least that was how it looked to me. There were dogs and people everywhere, swarming all around the brightly painted agility equipment. Two rings were set up side by side, with white rope separating them off. At the moment, a rangy brown-and-white dog was zipping around the course, while several people stood in the other ring, having some kind of consultation over one of the jumps. Off to the side, a tent city of lawn chairs and shaded dog crates lined the edge of the field.

"Wow," I said, taking it all in. "This is really something."

"It's great, isn't it?" Adam sounded distracted as he scanned the crowd. "I think I see my coach over there."

I had to scurry to keep up as he went striding off toward the crates and lawn chairs. "You have a coach?" I said. "I thought you were a coach."

"I am. But only for lower levels. So far." Adam tugged on Lark's leash as the border collie paused to sniff at the grass. "Phil helps me out with the girls when we compete at this level."

Soon we reached a cluster of people standing near the crates. Adam introduced one of them—a tall, balding man with crooked teeth and intelligent green eyes—as his coach.

"This is Lauren," he told Phil. "And that's Muckle. They're interested in maybe getting into agility, so they came along to check things out today."

Okay, that wasn't quite how I'd expected to be introduced. Still, maybe it wasn't realistic to think he'd refer to me as "Lauren, the love of my life" or "Lauren, my amazing new girlfriend" or even "Lauren, my date."

"Hi, Lauren," Phil said in a booming voice. "Welcome. I'm sure Adam will put you right to work."

He chortled, and the other people standing with him laughed too. I smiled politely, hanging on to Muckle as he tried to drag me over to say hi to the floppy-eared spaniel scrabbling at the wire door of the nearest crate.

"Easy, Muck," I said, scooping him up. "We've got to stay out of the way, okay?"

Muckle wiggled and barked in my ear, nearly deafening me. Noticing that Adam was wandering off, I smiled politely at Phil and the others and hurried to catch up.

"So what happens now?" I asked Adam.

I was hoping he'd say we could sit down together and watch the competition for a while. The images were already playing out in my head. Adam would tell me what was happening, I'd scoot a little closer on the bleachers to let someone by, his hand would drift to my knee . . .

Blinking, I realized he was walking off again. "Wait, what?" I called, scurrying after him.

"I said, I need to sign in." He squinted toward a large plastic tent at one end of the field. "It looks crowded over there. Can you hold the girls for a sec?"

Before I could say a word, I found myself holding two more leashes. As Adam walked off, Lark strained against her collar, whining softly.

"Um, it's okay, girl," I told her. "Stay here with me, okay?"

Shasta sat down, gazing at me with mild suspicion. Or maybe it was disdain; I couldn't tell. Meanwhile Lark started pacing, threatening to jerk the leash out of my hand with each pass. I looped the handle around my left wrist, hanging on to the other two leashes with my right hand while trying not to let the tote bag slide off my shoulder. Muckle seemed to find it great fun to follow Lark and sniff her butt every chance he got, which Lark mostly ignored.

It seemed to take forever for Adam to return, but finally he hurried over, looking vaguely tense. "We're up soon," he announced, reaching for Lark's leash.

I shivered as his hand brushed mine. Then I held out Shasta's leash, but Adam was already heading off without her. I shrugged and followed, with Muckle and Shasta trotting along beside me.

We caught up outside one of the rings. Adam was stroking Lark's head. He glanced up as I arrived.

"Listen, thanks for being here, Lauren," he said with a nervous smile. "It's nice to have a friendly face around. Nobody in my family is into dog sports that much, so I'm usually juggling both girls by myself. I'm really glad you came."

He looked so sincere, so vulnerable, that my heart melted. "Me too," I said. "It's fun."

We kept smiling at each other for a long moment. Once again, I felt that spark pass between us. He was so good-looking it was hard to believe he was real, and here, and on a date with me of all people. I drank in his eyes, his cheekbones, his broad shoulders . . .

Then a sharp whistle snapped me out of it. Adam blinked and straightened up, suddenly all business.

"We're on," he said.

"Good luck!" I called as he and Lark jogged away.

I dropped the tote bag on the grass at the edge of the ring and sat down beside it, being careful to keep hold of both leashes. Muckle was dashing back and forth in front of me, barking like crazy. Luckily, nobody around us seemed to mind, or even give him a second glance. Probably because a lot of their dogs were acting the same way.

Shasta was a little better; she mostly stood straining gently at the end of her leash, her eyes locked on Adam. I knew how she felt.

It was cool watching Adam and Lark do their thing. Lark moved so fast through the agility course that she was little more than a blur, and Adam was with her every step, directing her with hand motions and body language. I barely had time to take a breath before the round was over.

"Whoo-hoo!" I cheered, jumping to my feet. "Way to go, guys!"

Adam was grinning as he jogged back over. "Well, that didn't suck," he announced, grabbing Lark in a big hug. Shasta leaped toward him, wanting to get in on the action. Again, I knew how she felt. Feeling daring, I gave Adam a tentative pat on the shoulder as he rolled around with both border collies—oh, and Muckle, who had decided to join in the celebration as well.

"That was amazing," I said. "You two looked great out there."

"Thanks." He grinned up at me. "Just wait until you see Shasta go!" He patted the ground beside him. "Have a seat—we've got a few minutes before our turn, so we can hang out and watch some of the other rounds."

Now that was more like it. I sat down again, scooting as close to him as I dared—which wasn't particularly close, actually, since Shasta insisted on pressing up against him. Oh well. So far this "date" wasn't superromantic, but who needed flowers and soft music, really? I was getting to see Adam do what he did best, which was even better.

We spent the next few minutes living out my little fantasy from earlier. Well, parts of it, anyway. As several other dogs took their turns in the ring, Adam explained what was going on. A few times he even leaned close enough for our shoulders to brush—and he didn't seem to be in any hurry to pull away.

Then it was Shasta's turn. And Adam was right—she truly was impressive. She flew around the course so fast that the audience was cheering even before she finished. Adam was breathless when he came back.

"That was incredible!" I exclaimed as Muckle and Lark jumped around and barked, presumably congratulating Shasta in doggy language. "So did she win?"

"I'm not sure yet." Adam bit his lip and glanced at an older woman holding a clipboard nearby. "They'll announce it soon."

When the woman made the announcement, it turned out that Shasta had won—and Lark had come in second! Adam let out a whoop and pumped his fist, while both border collies went crazy. He hugged each of them in turn—then spun around and hugged me!

I gasped as he pulled me close, nearly squeezing the breath out of me. "We did it," he mumbled into my hair. "We did it!"

Now this was more like it! Okay, so it had taken a doggy triumph to get me some real up-close-and-personal contact. I'd take it!

"Yay," I said, finally realizing that I should be hugging him back. I wrapped my arms around him, loving the feel of being so close to him.

After a moment Adam pulled back slightly, smiling down at me. His face was so close that my breath caught in my throat. I found myself very focused on his lips. . . .

"Congratulations, dog boy," a sardonic voice said right behind me.

Adam let go of me and stepped back. "Oh. Hi, Tab."

I glanced back. A girl was standing there, arms crossed over her chest. She looked familiar. So did her dog, a Brittany that was already sniffing butts and noses with Muckle and the border collies. It was the girl from the dog park—the sporty-looking blonde I'd seen a couple of times now.

Now that I got a better look at her, I realized she was probably closer to Adam's age than to mine. She was also quite pretty, with hazel eyes and a deep tan. She looked me up and down in an appraising way.

"I've seen you around, haven't I?" she said. "I recognize your sheltie."

"Um, yeah. Dog park." I smiled uncertainly, wondering if that was how she knew Adam, too. They both seemed to spend a lot of time there.

"I'm Tabitha." She stuck out her hand. "Don't tell me Adam suckered another girl into wanting to hang out with him."

"Um, I'm Lauren." I shook her hand, not sure how to respond to the rest.

Adam frowned. "Lay off, Tab."

Tabitha ignored him, her pretty face twisting into a weird little smile. "I hope you're just in it for the agility tips or whatever, Lauren. Because if you're looking for anything else from this one, you're looking in the wrong place."

"Whatever, Tab." Adam sounded annoyed.

"Whatever yourself." She tossed him a smirk. "See you around, Lauren."

With that, she spun on her heel and marched off. The Brittany trotted after her. I had to hold Muckle back from following as well.

"What was that all about?" I asked Adam, a little freaked out by the bitterness in Tabitha's eyes when she'd looked at Adam.

He rolled his eyes. "Sorry about that. Ex-girlfriend," he said. "She never really understood my passion for dog sports."

"Oh." I didn't say anything else, though I couldn't help feeling uneasy. I mean, wasn't Tabitha a dog sport enthusiast herself? Why else would she be at the competition?

I didn't have much time to think about it. Phil was hurrying over to congratulate Adam and his dogs, followed by a stream of other well-wishers. Adam seemed to know everyone at the competition. Before I knew it, he was offering a ride home to a skinny guy with a goatee and a very large Doberman. A tiny, round woman with a corgi overheard and begged to tag along. Within minutes, we were all piling into the minivan.

It turned out the Doberman always insisted on riding shotgun, so I ended up in the far backseat with Muckle and the corgi. The other two humans sat in the middle with the border collies and chattered nonstop with Adam about the day's competition, only occasionally remembering to include me in the conversation.

I slumped in my seat, feeling vaguely disappointed. Still, no biggie—after we dropped the others off, Adam and I could get this date back on track. Maybe even recapture that moment that Tabitha had interrupted.

To my surprise, I soon realized Adam was pulling into my neighborhood. He stopped in front of my house and hurried around to let me out the side door.

"Oh," I said. "I thought we were going to grab something to eat?"

He looked sheepish. "Sorry, I thought we'd have more time. I still have to drive these guys home, then go get Jinx before flyball. Rain check?"

"Sure." I forced a smile.

Muckle and I watched from the sidewalk as the minivan pulled away in a cloud of exhaust. Okay, that definitely hadn't been the kind of first date I'd been expecting. I pulled out my phone, my finger already moving to the preset for Robert's number. Then I remembered: We still weren't speaking.

With a sigh, I stuck the phone back in my pocket and headed inside with Muckle.

Chapter ● Eighteen
Sunday funday

I spent most of Sunday morning moping around the house, wondering if Adam was going to call to ask me out again. Or just to say hi. Wasn't that what was supposed to happen? I wasn't sure, since I'd never been out on a real date before. Robert was right—the seventh-grade dance didn't count.

Speaking of Robert, I was really hoping he'd call too. I knew him—he had to be dying of curiosity wondering how things had gone yesterday. Wasn't that reason enough to get over himself and call to make up?

But when the phone finally rang, it wasn't either of them. It was Rachel.

"Hey, Lauren," she said. "I got your number off my phone from when you called before. Hope you don't mind."

"No, it's cool," I said. "What's up?"

"I was calling to see if you're doing anything this afternoon," she said. "Because Jamal and I and some other people from school might try to catch that zombie movie. Want to come?"

My first instinct was to say thanks but no thanks. I had very important sitting-by-the-phone plans, after all. And I didn't want to be a third wheel on their movie date.

But maybe that was the wrong attitude on both counts. Rachel had mentioned that "other people from school" were going too. If she and Jamal were testing the waters in a group setting, I wanted to support them. As for Adam and Robert? Sitting by the phone wouldn't make either of them call any faster.

Besides, I did want to see that movie. And even if Robert and I made up in the next ten seconds, there was still no way he'd go with me. While his hatred of horror was all-encompassing, zombie movies were probably his least favorite. Not only were they full of blood and guts, but tattered clothes as well, which was even more terrifying and horrific in Robert's eyes.

"Sure, that sounds great," I told Rachel. "Thanks. I'm really glad you called."

"I can't believe I'm the only one here who's never seen a single zombie movie," Rachel said as our little group walked away from the snack bar bearing drinks, candy, and popcorn. "Should I be worried?"

The group included me, Jamal, and the "other people from

school," who had turned out to consist of Jamal's friend Kenny and Rachel's friend Addie. Kenny was the guy Jamal had told me about—the one who'd tried to talk him into getting a big, tough, macho dog. He was pretty much the opposite of big, tough, and macho himself. Actually, he reminded me a little bit of Muckle. He was short and lean and happy-go-lucky and seemed physically incapable of remaining still and quiet for more than a millisecond.

Then there was Rachel's friend Addie, a bigmouthed, boisterous redhead with a loud laugh and a sarcastic wit. She wasn't anything like the type of friend I would have pictured Rachel having, but I liked her immediately.

At first I was afraid I'd feel like a fifth wheel in the group—after all, I was the only newbie, the only County Day kid, the not-quite-not-shy girl who didn't do well with strangers. But that concern faded after the first thirty seconds or so. All the MVHS kids were so nice and friendly and cool that they would have made a hermit feel comfortable hanging out with them.

"You'll love it, Rach. You haven't lived until you've watched a zombie eat a human brain." Addie elbowed me. "Am I right?"

"Totally." I grinned at Rachel. "Don't worry, nobody will be able to tell if you close your eyes at the gory parts."

"But don't be a wuss," Kenny put in, scooting forward to open the door for the rest of us. "You've got to watch the whole thing or it doesn't count."

"Doesn't count for what?" Jamal asked him.

Kenny shrugged and grinned. "Just doesn't count, dude."

"Good to know." Rachel walked past them into the theater.

I followed, mentally calculating the best way to make sure she and Jamal ended up sitting next to each other. So far, they weren't acting particularly couple-y. That wasn't really a surprise—Rachel was pretty shy, and Jamal probably didn't want to scare her off by being pushy. I figured sitting beside each other in the dark for a couple of hours might help them feel closer.

Somehow, though, it didn't work out that way. I tried to herd the two of them in ahead of me so they'd be stuck at the end of the row together, but then Rachel decided she needed to go out and grab more napkins. She wiggled out back past us, and somehow I ended up sitting between Jamal and Addie with Rachel out by the aisle beside Kenny. Oops.

"So this should be epic, right?" Jamal said, settling back in his seat and smiling at me. "I heard the special effects are killer."

"Yeah." I decided I might as well make productive use of this time to talk up Rachel a little more. "I hope Rachel likes it. She's really cool, isn't she?"

"Sure." Jamal tossed some popcorn into his mouth. Then he glanced over at me. "Oh, sorry. Want some?"

He held out the box. I took a couple of kernels. "Thanks. So do you and Rachel have many classes together?"

"Just English and gym." Jamal crunched on more popcorn. "So what classes do you take at County Day, Lauren?"

"Oh, just the usual." I tried to think of something else to say about Rachel. But at that moment, the lights dimmed and a cheer went up from the audience. For the next hour and a half, I forgot all about Rachel and Jamal—and even me and Adam—as I watched zombies eat the world.

"Seriously, how can you guys think about eating after watching that movie?" Rachel exclaimed, pushing away her menu.

We were all crowded into a booth at a local diner. This time I'd succeeded in arranging things so that Rachel and Jamal were seated together. They were squished next to each other on one side of the booth, with Addie on Rachel's other side. I was across from Jamal, next to Kenny.

Kenny licked his lips noisily. "The movie made me hungry," he declared. "Since there are no brains on the menu, I'll have to settle for a nice, juicy burger."

Addie laughed as Rachel shuddered. "Grow up, babe," she told her friend with a grin. "The movie wasn't real."

"Duh." Rachel rolled her eyes at Addie. "Anyway, I'm full from the popcorn. I'll just have a soda, I guess."

After we ordered, we spent the next few minutes talking about the movie. Then we moved on to other topics. Once again, I was amazed to find myself totally comfortable talking to these guys. Maybe I wasn't quite as not-quite-not-shy as I'd always thought. Maybe hanging out with someone so truly not shy as Robert had just let me get away with it. Or something. I was too busy having fun to psychoanalyze it, though I planned to think about it later.

I was disappointed when Kenny checked his watch and announced that he had to get going because he was supposed to babysit his little sister while his parents went out to dinner. Jamal was the only one with a car, so he offered to drive us all home. We all went out and piled into his car, which was a cool purple vintage Volkswagen hatchback. Somehow I ended up riding shotgun. I wished there was a way to switch places with Rachel, but I couldn't think of a way to do it that wasn't likely to be super obvious and embarrass her. And being easily embarrassed myself, I wasn't about to do that to her.

As Jamal headed down a side street leading to the local two-lane highway, Kenny leaned forward and poked him on the shoulder. "Why are you going this way, bro? It's shorter to take Main Street over to the west side of town."

"Can't." Jamal didn't take his eyes off the road. "I heard there was a bad accident over that way this morning. I figured I'd just avoid that mess by taking the highway to your place first and then circle back around."

"But there wasn't—" Addie cut herself off and shrugged. "Okay, if you say so, J. Hope you don't mind a long ride home, Lauren. Guess you'll be getting dropped off last."

"No problem. It's way better than taking the bus." I was a little disappointed; I'd been hoping he'd find an excuse to drop off the rest of us first so he could spend some alone time with Rachel. But traffic was traffic, so I didn't worry about it.

Soon we were saying good-bye to Kenny, and then to Rachel

and Addie, who both got out at Addie's house. "Nice meeting you," I said as Addie climbed out of the car.

"Yeah, ditto," she said. "We should do this again."

As we drove off, Jamal glanced at me. "They're nice, aren't they?"

"Definitely." My heart jumped. He looked so serious and thoughtful all of a sudden—was he thinking about how sweet and pretty Rachel was? Maybe even thinking of asking my advice about how to ask her out again? I just might have been better at this matchmaking thing than I thought.

We stayed silent while he pulled back out into traffic. Once we were cruising along, he looked over at me again. "I'm glad we got to see that movie together," he said. "There aren't many girls who appreciate a good brain-chewing scene."

I grinned. "Yeah. I'm thinking it's pretty much just me and Addie." Not wanting him to think I was criticizing Rachel, I quickly added, "But hey—everyone's got their own taste, right?"

"Sure." Jamal steered around a scrap of tire in the road. "Anyway, it was fun. We should do it again sometime."

I nodded, thinking about how Addie had just said the same thing. Would it happen? I hoped so. If Robert was never going to talk to me again, I'd need some new friends.

"How about Tuesday after class?" Jamal added.

I blinked, glancing over at him. "Sure. That sounds cool."

But now I wasn't really thinking about that anymore. Hearing Jamal mention our puppy class reminded me of Adam. Had he called? I'd switched off my phone ringer during the movie, and I'd forgotten to turn it back on at the diner. Pulling it out, I checked my messages. The only one was a text from Mom, wondering what time I'd be home.

Nothing from Adam. Nothing from Robert. Oh well.

"Cool." Jamal cleared his throat. "Um, sounds like a plan."

He spun the wheel to make the turn onto my street. When he pulled to the curb in front of my house, he cut the engine and turned to face me.

"So this was a lot of fun," he said with a smile. He leaned a little closer. "Seriously. I'm glad we finally got to—"

He was cut off by the sound of barking. I recognize Muckle's high-pitched yapping immediately and had a moment of panic. What was he doing outside? Had Mom finally snapped and kicked him out of the house after yet another accident involving her stupid rug?

That was indeed Muckle racing around the side of the house onto the front lawn, but he wasn't alone. "Whoa," I said, my brain struggling to make sense of what I was seeing. Or rather who I was seeing, clinging on to the other end of the leash. "This is weird."

"What?" Jamal asked.

"That's my mom—and it looks like she's walking Muckle." I blinked a few times, wondering if all the grease, sugar, and caffeine I'd just consumed was making me hallucinate or something. "She never does that. She's never done that."

But she was doing it now. Mom looked breathless and a little overwhelmed as Muckle dragged her toward Jamal's car, barking nonstop.

"Oh, dear," she exclaimed, tugging on the leash. "He's awfully strong for such a small dog, isn't he? You'd better get out here and grab him before he scratches your friend's car, Lauren."

"Coming." Rolling my eyes at Jamal, I hopped out of the car. "You didn't have to walk him, Mom. I was going to do it as soon as I got home."

"Well, he was actually behaving nicely today while you were out. I didn't want him to pee on the rug and ruin everything." As soon as I took the leash, Mom leaned down to peer in at Jamal. "Hello, young man," she said. "Thanks for getting Lauren home safely."

"Uh, you're welcome, ma'am." Jamal glanced at me. "I'd better get home and walk my own puppy. See you Tuesday, Lauren?"

"Yeah." I was too busy wondering if the aliens had come along and turned my mother into a pod person—a pod person who actually seemed to like Muckle—to pay much attention to Jamal. "See you Tuesday."

Chapter ✺ Nineteen
Surprises

was in a mildly cranky mood when I arrived at school on Monday. Partly because the school bus had been extra smelly and crowded that morning. But mostly because Adam had never called or even texted. What did that mean? Hadn't he had a good time on Saturday?

When I neared my locker, I saw Robert waiting there. He rushed over and flung his arms around me.

"I can't stand it anymore, Parker," he exclaimed. "I hate fighting with you. I absolutely insist we make up right this second, and I won't take no for an answer. I swear, I'll hold my breath until I turn blue if I have to. And you know I don't look good in blue."

I hugged him back, too surprised and relieved to do anything else. My mood soared. "Okay," I said. "Done. We're officially made up."

"Thank God." After one last squeeze, he let me go and stepped back to survey me. "You look good. Although I wouldn't have suggested that belt with those shoes."

I gave him a shove. "Never mind the fashion tips—I've been dying to tell you about Saturday."

"Saturday?" He raised an eyebrow. "You mean your date with Dog Boy?"

I quickly spun my combination lock, grabbing a notebook I needed and tucking it into my bag. "What else? So we went to the agility competition. Which was actually super fun . . ."

I went on to give him a summary of my day at the agility competition with Adam. When I finished, Robert didn't look terribly impressed.

"So he dropped you off first? Lame," he pronounced. "I'm telling you, Lauren, this guy seems completely clueless. You can do better."

Better than a hot older guy with an Irish accent? Better than Adam, the most amazing guy ever? I doubted it. But I was too glad to be talking to Robert again to get into an argument so soon, so I decided to let it drop.

"So did you study for the French test?" I asked instead.

That did the trick. We quizzed each other on verb conjugations until the bell rang.

"Are you sure the eye shadow isn't too much?" I flipped down the Volvo's sun visor and peered at myself in the mirror. It was Tuesday afternoon, and we'd just pulled into the Maple View Shopping Center.

"It's perfect." Robert found a parking space right in front of PetzBiz. "Very subtle. Trust me, you look gorge."

"Okay. Thanks." Given his comments about Adam the day before, I was still surprised by how enthusiastic Robert had been about helping me get ready for today's puppy class. But I wasn't going to worry about it. He was probably just trying to make up for missing out on helping me get ready on Saturday. Anyway, he loved makeovers, no matter what the reason.

When I reached the training ring, Jamal and Rachel were already there. Jamal spotted me first and patted the empty seat beside him.

"Hey!" he called out with his usual friendly smile. "Saved you a seat, Lauren."

"Thanks." I sat down while Muckle greeted the other puppies. I couldn't help noticing that Jamal looked extra good today. Instead of his usual jeans, he was wearing khakis and a button-down shirt. I even thought I detected a hint of cologne. Was he trying to impress Rachel?

I didn't have time to think about it much. Adam was hurrying toward us.

"Lauren," he said. "Hi. Talk a sec?"

My heart thumped so loudly I was sure everyone could hear it. "Sure."

I handed Muckle's leash to Rachel and followed Adam to an

empty part of the ring. He turned to face me, his hands stuffed into his jeans pockets.

"So," he said, clearing his throat. "I wanted to thank you for keeping me company on Saturday."

"Oh." Keeping him company? Okay, that was kind of a weird way to put it, but maybe it was an Irish thing. "You're welcome. I mean, it was fun."

"Yeah? You had a good time?" He looked pleased. "Because I was going to take my dogs to the dog park today after class. Want to come? They need some exercise, and I'd love the company."

"Okay!" I wanted to do a he-asked-me-out-again dance right there and then but managed to control myself. "Sounds great!"

When I returned to my seat, Jamal smiled at me. "So, we're still on for today after class, right?"

"Huh?" Belatedly, I remembered that we'd made plans. "Oh, wow, I totally forgot. Um, I can't make it today." I flashed him what I hoped was a properly apologetic smile, though my mind was so filled with Adam that I could hardly focus on anything else. "Sorry! I'm sure you guys will all have fun, though. Rain check?"

"Yeah," he said slowly. "Sure. No problem."

Just then Adam called for class to begin. I quickly texted Robert, telling him he wouldn't need to pick me up after class.

Then I just sat there, drinking in the sight of Adam. How many dates would it take before I could start calling him my boyfriend? Did he have to kiss me first? If so, maybe we could work on that this afternoon. I spent most of the rest of class daydreaming about that, only vaguely aware of what I was doing. Luckily, Jamal didn't have much to say for once, and of course Rachel was always pretty quiet. Muckle also behaved himself for the most part.

Before long I found myself back in Adam's minivan with all three of his dogs. Plus Muckle, of course. We chatted about that day's class during the drive over to the dog park, then unloaded the beasts and headed in.

I wasn't sure what I was expecting. But the next hour wasn't it. There was no hand-holding, no dreamy looks, and certainly no kissing. Instead I spent about half an hour trying to hang on to a very worked-up Muckle's leash while we watched Adam run around the big lawn with his dogs. It was tempting to let Muckle run with the other three, but I was afraid I'd never catch him again even with Adam's help.

After that, we headed into one of the agility enclosures. Okay, that was more like it, right? Maybe Adam would help me with Muckle again, our hands touching, our bodies close together. . . .

But no. This time he mostly focused on Lark, trying to get her jumps cleaner. Or something. After twenty minutes watching the border collie take the jumps over and over, I kind of tuned out what Adam was saying.

I tried not to lose heart, though. Adam had said his dogs needed exercise. After they got it, he'd be able to focus on me. Right? Otherwise, why would he have bothered to invite me?

The thought made me feel slightly more hopeful. When

Adam finally released Lark and turned toward me, I wet my lips and pasted a pleasant smile on my face.

"That last run was better, eh?" he said, a little breathless. "She's coming along."

"Yeah, she looks great," I said brightly. "Looks like she wore you out, though. Sit?" I patted the bench beside me.

He sat down. Shasta immediately ran over and buried her face in his lap. He fondled her head, smoothing back her ears. Uh-oh. I shouldn't be jealous of a dog, right?

What would Robert tell me to do if he was here? Okay, he'd probably start blabbing about how Adam was too clueless to bother with. But if he was in the mood to help, he'd tell me to go for it, right?

I scooted a little closer on the bench, until our shoulders bumped. Adam was still playing with Shasta's ears and didn't seem to notice. Would he notice if I grabbed his head and planted a wet one right on his lips? Probably, but I definitely didn't have the guts to go that far.

"So," I said instead. "This is nice, huh?"

"What?" He glanced over. "I mean, yeah, it's great. Nice to have company." He laughed. "I mean human company, eh?"

He was finally looking at me now, his blue eyes friendly. And close. So close. Really, how hard would it be to lean forward a bit, close my eyes . . . ?

"Adam! I thought I saw you in here!" a loud voice boomed out.

I jumped back, as flustered as if we really had been kissing instead of me just imagining it. A paunchy, middle-aged man in an expensive designer Windbreaker had just let himself into the enclosure. A dog came with him—a large, half-grown Irish setter that immediately bounded up to Shasta and knocked her over.

The man glanced that way. "Easy, Rascal," he called mildly. Then he hurried over to us. His eyes swept over me, and he gave me the briefest of nods before focusing on Adam.

"Hi, Mr. Kearns," Adam greeted the man, standing and shaking hands. "How's it going?"

"Listen," Mr. Kearns said. "Rascal's still having some trouble playing nicely with others. Some woman just went off on me because he scared her Peekaboo or Sneakapoo or something." He rolled his eyes. "Since you're here anyway, got time for a session?"

I'd been watching the dogs, a little concerned. Rascal had Muckle cornered over by the A-frame. Adam's dogs were milling around nearby, all of them seeming wary of the newcomer, though Jinx occasionally darted forward and barked at him.

But now I focused back in on the conversation. Adam was already nodding.

"Of course, Mr. Kearns," he said. "Why don't you grab him and get him back on the leash? I'll be with you in a sec."

The older man hurried off. Adam turned to me with an apologetic look.

"Sorry, Lauren," he said quietly. "This guy's one of my richest clients, and he's not a super-patient guy, if you know what I mean. I can't afford to turn him down."

I shot a look across the ring at Mr. Kearns, who was chasing his dog around and under the dog walk. It might have been a comical scene if I wasn't standing here getting blown off because of it. Then I returned my gaze to Adam. Suddenly I was over it. Maybe it was the boredom, or maybe I'd finally come to my senses. Either way, I wasn't particularly hurt or upset or even surprised. Just numb.

"Whatever," I said. "That's fine. Go ahead."

"Thanks, Lauren." He flashed me a brief smile, then hurried off to help Mr. Kearns collect his dog. Soon they were gone, along with Jinx and the border collies.

That left Muckle and me alone in the enclosure. After a moment of distressed barking and pacing when his friends left without him, Muckle went back to running around, sniffing at stuff. I was sitting there staring at him when the gate opened again. It was Tabitha.

"Hi." She came up to me while her dog trotted over to say hi to Muckle. "Sorry, I swear I'm not some crazy stalker. But I was in the next pen, and I saw what just happened." Her mouth twisted into a sympathetic half smile. "It looked like you just got Adamed."

I blinked at her. "Adamed?"

"Uh-huh." Tabitha sank down on the bench beside me. "Been there. Big-time. When I met Adam, I thought I'd won the lottery. I mean, he's great-looking, a nice guy, and into dogs just like me. What could be better, right?"

"Yeah," I muttered. "Sounds familiar."

She sighed. "The thing is, Adam is a great trainer who truly loves dogs. He's even a great guy in some ways. But he's a lousy boyfriend."

"I don't get it." The numbness was wearing off a little, making me feel bleak and raw. "Why's he like that?"

"Got me. He's just obsessive by nature, I guess, and way focused on his goals. And right now girls aren't really a part of that." She shrugged. "Too bad. He is awfully cute."

After chatting with Tabitha for another few minutes, I felt better. Slightly, anyway. At least I knew it wasn't me. Not that it was going to be easy to get over this either way.

It was only after Tabitha had left that I realized something. Not only had Adam run out on our date with barely a second thought, but he'd also ditched me with no ride home. Nice. I tried to work up some righteous indignation about that, but I mostly just felt sad as I called Robert to come pick me up.

When I climbed into the Volvo with Muckle twenty minutes later, Robert was scowling. "What's with you?" I asked. "I thought you'd be happy. You said he was no good, and you were right. You love being right."

"I can't believe you," he snapped. "Jamal went to a lot of trouble to set up today's date. I can't believe you just blew it off!"

"Huh?" All I could do was stare at him. "What are you talking about?"

He glared back at me, ignoring Muckle, who was licking his chin in greeting. "You were supposed to go out with Jamal after puppy class today. I had no idea you'd skipped out on it until I noticed your text."

"Hold on, back up a sec," I said. "I didn't have a date with Jamal. I mean, yeah, we'd talked about maybe getting together again after class, but that was just a group thing." I hesitated. "Um, wasn't it?"

"No," Robert spat out. "It wasn't. Jamal tracked me down online yesterday, wanting to find out what you like to do. He was super nervous about it—really wanted to impress you."

My mind spun, trying to take in this new development. "So it wasn't a group thing."

"Catch up, genius." Robert pushed Muckle off his lap and started the car. "I thought we'd covered that part. Yes, today was supposed to be just the two of you. On a private picnic with all your favorite foods."

"A picnic?" I gasped. "I always thought that was the most romantic date ever."

"Duh. I know." Robert shot me a sour look. "Who do you think suggested the idea? He went all out, too—figured out the perfect spot overlooking Spring Creek, ordered the food, downloaded some new stuff on his iPod—that was thanks to me too. For a cool guy, he has some pretty questionable tastes in music."

"Oh, man." I felt horrible. Had Jamal really done all that to impress me? He was so sweet! Not to mention cool, and funny, and good-looking . . .

Suddenly it dawned on me that maybe I shouldn't have been

so quick to write him off as not my type. Here I'd been pining after exotic, not-so-actually-amazing Adam, when maybe my real dream guy had been right under my nose the whole time!

Robert still looked cranky. "Poor guy is probably down by the creek right now, cleaning up the blanket and stuff he set out there this morning to surprise you."

I grabbed his arm so abruptly that he swerved halfway onto the shoulder. "Quick," I ordered. "You have to take me there! To the picnic spot, I mean. Maybe it's not too late. I can apologize, see if he still wants to hang out, maybe have that picnic after all."

"Really?" Robert brightened. "So you do like him. I knew it!"

"I didn't," I replied. "I mean I didn't know I did. Or something. We can figure it out later, okay? Now hurry—we don't want to miss him!"

My heart raced along with the Volvo. It seemed to take forever to get there, but finally Robert pulled off the road at a scenic overlook. There were a couple of other cars parked there.

"He's here!" I cried, staring at one of the cars—a distinctive grape-colored Volkswagen. "I'm not too late! Where's the picnic spot?"

"Go look over the wall," Robert instructed. "You should be able to see it down the hill to the left."

"Oh, great." I undid my seat belt. "So you set it up so the whole world could stop here and gawk at us?"

"Just go!"

I jumped out of the car and hurried over to the wall that kept scenic-overlookers from tumbling down the steep bank to the creek. A flash of movement caught my eye down to the left, and I leaned forward eagerly.

Then I gasped. It was Jamal—locked in an embrace with Rachel!

Chapter ✷ Twenty
Fallout

stumbled back to the Volvo and clambered in, grabbing Muckle's collar to keep him from leaping out. "Get out of here," I told Robert. "It's too late. I blew it."

"What do you mean?" He stared at me. "I thought you said that was his car."

"It is." I shook my head. "But I'm an idiot. I just realized who my real dream guy is, but now another girl has him. And it's all my fault—why couldn't I see it before this?"

"Because you were blinded by Adam's beauty." Robert sounded sympathetic. "But what are you talking about? What other girl?"

"Rachel. I just saw her and Jamal down there. Together." I grimaced at the image now seared into my brain. "They were looking pretty chummy, if you know what I mean. And that part's definitely my fault. I've been pushing the two of them together for, like, the past week because I felt bad about not liking Jamal back." I hugged Muckle, who was sitting quietly in my lap for once. "At least I didn't think I liked him back," I added, my voice muffled by the puppy's fur.

Robert didn't say anything. Instead he started the engine and pulled out of the overlook. He liked a dramatic scene, but I guessed even he didn't want to witness my humiliation if Jamal came up there and saw me right then.

"I can't believe I was so stupid," I said as we hit the highway. "I mean, I thought Jamal was cool from the first time I met him. I just never thought of him that way, you know? Despite the fact that he was actually available and seemed to be interested in me. Unlike every other guy I've ever had a crush on, including Adam." I grimaced. "Now that I'm coming to my senses, it's too late. And I can't even hate Rachel for it, because she's so awesome too."

"I'm so sorry, sweetie," Robert said. "I truly am."

"I know." I buried my face in Muckle's furry coat, allowing a few tears to soak into it. I felt like an idiot for crying, but then again, I was an idiot. I didn't deserve a guy like Jamal.

Which was a good thing, because I didn't have him.

I was walking Muckle after school the next day when my phone buzzed in my pocket. Fishing it out, I was surprised to see that it was Rachel.

"Hello?" I said, wondering if I'd somehow mentally summoned the call. After all, I'd spent the past twenty-four hours telling myself over and over again that I was happy for Jamal and Rachel. That they were both great people who'd be great together. Better than me and Jamal, probably. Maybe.

"Lauren? It's Rachel." It was hard to miss the snippy tone of her voice. Which didn't seem like her. "We need to talk."

"Okay," I said cautiously. "What's up?"

"It's about Jamal."

I gulped. Could she tell I liked her new boyfriend now? But how? I hadn't seen either of them since the overlook, and I was positive neither of them had seen me there. And I certainly hadn't shown much interest in Jamal before that. Unfortunately.

"Jamal?" I echoed, playing dumb.

"Yes, Jamal," she snapped. "I've never seen him like this. You really hurt him, ditching him like that yesterday."

"I know," I said. "I realize that now. It was a mistake; I didn't realize we were supposed to—but so what?" I interrupted myself. "He's with you now, right? You can comfort him." Okay, it came out a little more bitter than intended. I couldn't help it.

"Huh?" This time Rachel sounded confused. "He's not with me right now."

"No, I mean like *with you* with you. You know—boyfriend-girlfriend?" I took a deep breath. "I saw you two yesterday. At the overlook? You were hugging. Or something. I didn't stick around to watch," I added hastily, not wanting to sound like a Peeping Tom.

"What? But we didn't . . ." There was a moment of silence. Then she laughed. "Oh, wait—you saw us hugging? It must have been when I came to help him clean up the picnic he set up for you. And I was trying to make him feel better about being blown off by you."

"You mean—I thought—but—," I stammered, trying to take in what she was telling me.

She didn't let me finish. "Jamal is a lot more sensitive than he seems," she said. "I've gotten to know him better this year, and I never realized it before. A lot of girls are always after him, but he never really went for it with anyone—until he met you. He put himself out there for you, big-time."

"H-he did?" How was I supposed to feel about that? From her tone, I couldn't quite tell.

"Uh-huh. But now I'm afraid he might have given up on you. And that's a shame. You guys would've been good together. Everyone could see it." She paused. "Except you, apparently."

"Yeah. Looks that way." Now I knew how to feel. Terrible. This was a guy I had stuff in common with. Unlike Adam. I'd realized by now that the only thing I had in common with him was an interest in dogs.

Jamal was different. We had fun when we were together. He was easy to talk to, easy to be with. He made me laugh. He liked horror movies. He got along with Robert. I liked his friends, too—at least the ones I'd met so far.

But it didn't matter. "Guess I blew it, huh?"

"I guess," Rachel said softly. "Anyway, I just thought you should know how I felt. Sorry, I'm not usually so mean."

"I know. And it's okay." I said good-bye and hung up, then immediately hit Robert's number. I was sure he'd yell at me too, but I still wanted to talk to him. Maybe he could help me figure out a way to make this okay.

But I doubted it. Even Robert's powers might not be up to that task.

By Friday morning, I wasn't feeling much better about things. I moped through breakfast and barely had the energy to slick on some lip gloss after I got dressed. What was the point in trying to look good? Nobody cared. Especially me.

When I heard Robert's car horn outside, I hurried downstairs—and almost tripped over Muckle, who was dancing around by the front door. Oops.

"Oh no," I blurted out. "I haven't walked you yet!"

Mom stepped in from the living room just in time to hear me. "It's all right," she said, reaching for the leash hanging on the coat closet doorknob. "Robert's already here. I'll take the dog out."

"You will?" I blinked at her. "But I'm supposed to—I mean, you said—I mean, I thought—"

Mom snapped the leash onto Muckle's collar. "You've really stepped up to the plate lately, Lauren," she said as she straightened up. "Don't think your father and I haven't noticed. I mean, I haven't been to the dry cleaner's all week—if this keeps up, they won't recognize me anymore!" She winked.

Yes, winked! And smiled! While talking about Muckle!

"B-but—," I stammered.

Mom wasn't listening. Because she was—drumroll, please— petting Muckle! Yes, she'd just leaned down again and given him a pat on his furry little head!

Aliens. It had to be the aliens. Or maybe not. It was only then that I realized Muckle hadn't had an accident in the house in three full days. I'd been too distracted to pay much attention to stuff like that, what with the whole romantic disaster my life had become lately. But it obviously hadn't escaped my parents' attention. And maybe Mom didn't mind having a dog around so much when he wasn't ruining the decor every five minutes.

Robert's horn blared again. "You'd better go, Lauren," Mom said. "You don't want to be late."

"Um, okay. Thanks, or whatever," I mumbled, still too confused to be coherent.

At least something good had come out of this whole situation, I thought as I grabbed my stuff and headed outside. Adam might not be my dream guy after all, but he was one heck of a puppy trainer.

"I've got an idea," Robert said as we drove out of the school park- ing lot that afternoon. "You need to snap out of your funk. What better way than the Disguise Game?"

I groaned. "Not in the mood."

He ignored me. "I was thinking we dress up as serious athletes and go hang out somewhere. Drink some smoothies. You know. Do whatever it is that serious athletes do when they're not athleting and stuff."

I rolled my eyes. "If we can pass ourselves off as serious athletes, we'd truly be the masters of disguise."

"Good. So you'll do it?" He grinned.

"I didn't say that," I protested. But it was no use. Robert's mind was made up, and that was that. It was easier to go along with him than try to fight it.

An hour later we were back in the car, this time decked out in our disguises. Robert was wearing tennis whites and aviators, while I was dressed in vintage eighties baggy gray gym shorts and leg warmers that were straight out of *Flashdance*. Even Muckle was in on the act this time—Robert had tied a jaunty bandanna around his neck.

"I feel like an idiot." I fingered the slick polyester fabric of my shorts. "Where are we going in this crazy getup, anyway—1985, perhaps?"

"If that's a *Flashdance* reference, the original film came out in '83," Robert informed me.

"Thanks, Captain Trivia. But seriously, where are we going? I don't want anyone I know to see me in this."

"You'll see." He smiled mysteriously and kept driving.

I slumped down in my seat, figuring it didn't matter who saw me looking like an eighties outcast. My life was over anyway. Well, my love life, anyway. Because I was pretty sure I was never going to get over this. First finding out that Adam, the guy I'd thought was so perfect for me, was actually . . . not. And then to have the whole Jamal fiasco happen on top of that? It was too much. Maybe I'd become a nun or something.

My gloomy thoughts circled around in my brain like buzzards over roadkill as Robert drove on, humming along with the radio. After a while, I snapped out of it just enough to realize we'd been on the road for a long time. Sitting up, I saw that we were entering a neighboring town.

"Seriously, where are we going?" I asked.

"Somewhere we'll fit right in with our disguises," he replied. A moment later he turned the car into the driveway of the local high school. "Come with me."

I thought about refusing, but again, it didn't seem worth the effort. So I climbed out of the car and let Muckle drag me along after Robert, who was walking so quickly he almost did seem like an athlete.

"Wait up, will you?" I grumbled.

We rounded the corner of the school building and came in sight of the athletic fields. Some sort of event was going on out on the track—brightly clad people were bouncing on their toes and doing stretches and stuff.

"What is this?" I asked, suddenly suspicious.

Robert grabbed my arm and dragged me forward. "I told you," he said. "Somewhere I thought we'd fit in."

Muckle barked and lunged forward, his tail wagging eagerly. He was staring at someone jogging by on the track a dozen yards away. The runner wasn't looking our way, but I recognized him instantly.

"Jamal!" I blurted out, my body going hot and cold in turns. I whirled on Robert. "You knew he'd be here!"

Robert grinned. "Guilty."

"I have to get out of here before he sees me!" I was so furious I could have strangled Robert with my bare hands. How could he humiliate me like this? Rachel had pretty much told me Jamal was over me. What would he think if he saw me here?

It was all too much. I took off for the parking lot. Or tried to, anyway. At that moment, Muckle lunged toward Jamal again, and the leash slipped out of my hand.

"Muckle, no!" I cried. "Oh, man . . ."

Muckle took off toward Jamal, barking gleefully. I sprinted after him.

Jamal finally heard the crazy dog heading his way and looked up. His eyes widened when he recognized Muckle, then saw me running after the puppy.

"Lauren?" he said. "What are you—oof!"

Muckle had just reached him. Jamal was so busy staring at me that he tripped over the bouncing puppy—and fell right on me, pretty much.

I braced myself as he stumbled into me, catching him by the arms. "Are you okay?" I asked as he clutched at me and Muckle continued to dance around us like the goofy puppy he was.

Jamal caught his balance, but he didn't pull away. I didn't either. We just stood there, my hands on his arms, staring at each other. His gaze flicked briefly to my shorts and leg warmers. "Um, nice outfit," he mumbled.

Oh, the heck with it. I was already about as humiliated as a girl could be. What did I have to lose? I might as well go for it.

"I'm sorry," I blurted out. "I was a clueless jerk. I didn't realize you were asking me out the other day, or I never would have ditched you like that, I swear. I was crushing on Adam and kind of lost track of everything else, but then I realized he's not what I thought he was, and then Robert told me what was going on. I mean, that what I thought was just a group get-together was supposed to be, you know, a date. But by then it was too late, and when I saw you and Rachel together at the overlook I thought something was going on between you, and so I took off again, and I'm a total idiot, and I've never really had a boyfriend before, so I don't know how to do any of this—not that that's an excuse, but you know—and I guess I thought you weren't my type at first, but then . . ."

I babbled on for what felt like a year, probably making less and less sense all the time as I tried to explain what had happened and why. Jamal stood there and listened, his expression impossible to read.

". . . and anyway, Rachel told me everything, but I figured it was too late. Which is too bad." I took a deep breath. "Because, well, I finally realized I, you know, like you."

I braced myself again, emotionally this time. What would happen now? I had no idea; I'd never done anything like this before. Whatever happened, I was proud of myself. So nervous I was afraid I might puke, but proud.

"You do?" Jamal's eyes lit up.

"Um, yeah." I held my breath.

One corner of his mouth quirked up in a funny little half smile. "Well, as I guess you figured out, I kinda like you too."

"Like?" I hesitated. "Or liked? As in past tense?"

"Like." He smiled all the way then. "As in present tense." The smile faded. "But wait, are you sure you don't like Adam anymore? He is a pretty cool guy."

"Maybe. But I'm definitely over him."

"Oh. That's good." He looked happier again.

After that we just stood there for a while, grinning at each other, neither of us knowing what to say or do next. Realizing I wasn't sure what had happened to Robert, I glanced over my shoulder. There he was—standing with Rachel, both of them staring at us with big, goofy grins on their faces. Oh, great. Just when I thought I couldn't be more embarrassed.

Muckle let out a sharp bark, his ears pricked toward something across the track. Oops. I realized he was still loose.

"Muck," I said. "Stay!"

I leaned down and grabbed his leash. Muckle barked again and bowed down, inviting me to play. Then he took off, racing around behind Jamal.

"Whoa!" Jamal exclaimed as the leash tightened around his lower legs. "Easy, Muck . . ."

This time when he fell into me I decided to follow Robert's advice for once—be brave, grab life by the throat, go for it. I wrapped my arms around Jamal's back, steadying him. Then I stood on my tiptoes, leaned forward, and pressed my lips to his.

His eyes widened in surprise. But he recovered quickly. A second later his arms were pulling me even closer as he kissed me back.

My eyes drifted shut. I was so lost in the kiss that I barely heard Muckle barking, or Robert whooping. It was all about me and Jamal now. Maybe he wasn't the type of guy I'd been dreaming about all these years.

But I knew now that he was definitely the guy of my dreams.

A. DESTINY is the coauthor of the Flirt series. She spends her time reading books, writing, and watching sweet romance movies. She will always remember her first kiss.

CATHERINE HAPKA has written more than one hundred books for children and adults, as a ghostwriter for series as well as original titles. She lives in Pennsylvania.

TURN THE PAGE FOR MORE FLIRTY FUN.

Ever since I was a little girl, I've dreamed of being a star on the flying trapeze. Most girls grow up wanting to be a ballerina or a princess. Most of them stop dreaming once they become teenagers. Not me. Ever since my parents took me to see my first circus show, I knew that was the life for me. Watching the aerialist flip and twirl in midair, listening to all that applause . . . I couldn't think of anything better. Everyone in the tent was watching, everyone wanted to be them. And someday, I wanted to be the one who was the source of all that admiration.

Of course, it's hard to run away and join the circus when your parents are dead set on you going to college—probably for something practical like accounting or dentistry. It also doesn't help when you live in Middle of Nowhere, Missouri.

So the fact that I'm here, standing in front of a sign reading THE KARAMAZOV SISTERS' TRAVELING CIRCUS: FIRST ANNUAL YOUTH CAMP is a pretty big deal. I mean, the Karamazov sisters have been coming to town every summer for as long as I can remember. But for them to have a circus camp? One where I could learn flying trapeze and become a star? It almost seems too good to be true.

"You owe us for the rest of your life," my mom says. "Remember this, Jennifer, when you're picking out our nursing home."

I grin at her and Dad.

"I know," I say. Neither of them really wants me to go to camp. I think they would rather I just stay at home and play video games with my friends like I have every other spring break. But I'm fifteen. It's time to start reaching for my dreams. And a weeklong camp doing circus is the best way to begin. I know, deep down, that this is going to be life changing. This is the point in my story where I finally flourish. At least, that's what I've been telling myself right up to now.

Actually, being here is starting to make me worry that I might have been wrong about all that.

The camp is held on the community college campus. We stand in the parking lot in front of the main office, and it's hard to believe that I've biked past here more often than I can count. The place is entirely different, and not just because there are dozens of teenagers my age walking around with their parents.

There are semitrucks parked outside the gym and tents being put up. None of them are quite as big as the big top for the Karamazov show, but they're all genuine circus tents, stripes and stars and all. My heart leaps when I see the structure they're assembling a little farther off, out on the soccer field. It's not complete, but I know without a doubt what it is.

"Looks like that's where you'll be spending all of your time," Dad says, noticing my gaze. He's got my suitcase balanced against his leg. I didn't pack much, not since it was only for a week. And besides, gymnastics clothes—all new, all part of my early birthday present—pack up pretty easily.

I don't actually have words. I stare at the flying trapeze rig, a little starstruck, and nod.

I'm not left to stare long. A girl who looks like she's a college supermodel comes up to us. She's got long brown hair in a ponytail and impeccable makeup. Her green eyes match the T-shirt she's wearing, and her shorts barely reach her thighs. She's gorgeous. What's more, I've seen her before; she's one of the hoop aerialists for the show.

"Hi," she says, stopping in front of me. She holds out her hand with a warm smile. "I'm Leena. Are you here for the camp?"

I nod as I take her hand, unable to peel my eyes from her. Just last summer I was watching this girl perform amazing stunts on a hoop dangling a dozen feet in the air. And now she's shaking my hand! It's like meeting a celebrity, only this star's hands are covered in calluses, and there are a few faint bruises on her forearms and calves.

"Did you get attacked by a lion?" my dad asks. I shoot him

the angriest look I can manage. I haven't even gotten to introduce myself yet.

The girl raises an eyebrow, then looks to her arms and laughs.

"No, though that would make for a better story. These are just part of the gig. The battle scars of being an aerialist. Turns out hanging from a metal hoop hurts." She laughs again. "I'm sorry, I shouldn't be scaring you off. Especially not before getting your name."

"Jennifer," I say. "Jennifer Hayes. And these are my parents."

Leena shakes my mom and dad's hands, and I can tell from my mom's expression that she's not too happy about the fact that this girl is covered in bruises from being in the circus. At least she doesn't say anything; she's a little more tactful than Dad.

"Nice to meet you, Jennifer," Leena says. "Is this your first time doing circus arts?"

I nod. Even though she's at least twenty-one, there isn't any condescension in her voice. She's looking at me like even if I'm not currently her equal, I might be. Someday.

"Well, this is going to be an intense week. I hope you're ready for it. You look like you're a natural, though—nothing to worry about." She gives me a grin. "Anyway, registration's right inside the door. They'll get you sorted and into your dorm. I'll see you at the opener in an hour."

She nods to my parents and then walks off, toward another group of kids milling about as aimlessly as I probably appear to be.

"She seems nice," my dad says when she's out of earshot.

"Yeah," I say. I'm still glowing. A natural? She thinks I could be a natural? "Really smooth, by the way. Thanks for trying to embarrass me."

"I wasn't," he replies. "I just wanted to make sure she hadn't been hurt, that's all. I mean, I'm entrusting you to her care. If there's anything bad going on behind the scenes . . ."

"I know, I know." I pat him on the arm. "You gotta look out for your little girl."

"You're sure you want to do this aerial thing?" Mom asks. She keeps glancing back to Leena, no doubt wondering if there are more bruises we can't see. "It looks . . . painful."

"Totally sure," I say. "Besides, she does hoop. I'm going to do flying trapeze—the only thing I have to worry about are bad calluses. Come on. Before registration closes."

I head toward the door. They stay behind, but only for a moment. Then they're following at my heels, the wheels of my suitcase rumbling on the pavement. The sky is clear, it's not crazy hot outside, and I've just met one of my new coaches—who I've been watching for years. I don't think this day could get any better if it tried.

Registration is quick and simple; not ten minutes later, my parents are hugging me outside the door to my dorm, which is actually just one of the rooms in on-campus housing. There isn't any tear shedding, not like when I went to my first and only summer camp four years ago. I mean, I'm only here a week, and my house is only a few miles away. I think I can cope. Or, if I'm being really honest here, I think *they* can cope.

"Call if you need anything," Dad says.

"And make sure you text us when you know the time for your show. We wouldn't miss it for the world."

"I will," I say. I hug them both. "Love you."

Then, just like that, they're gone. Vanished down the hall. And I'm sitting in my room, staring at a suitcase of leotards and shorts and sweatpants, about to start the first day of the rest of my life. I've done it. I've basically run away and joined the circus, at least for a week. I grin. No more "Jennifer Hayes, girl no one really pays attention to." It's time for "Jennifer Hayes, high-flying circus star" to take the stage.

The door opens again a few minutes later, when I'm putting my clothes away in one of the drawers. I glance over. The first thing I notice is fire-engine red. Then I realize the shock of red is attached to the head of a girl. I blink hard. Yep, her hair is bright red, the same color as the striped red-and-black stockings sticking out of her camo skirt.

"Hi," she says the moment she's in the room. "You must be my roommate. I'm Riley."

"Jennifer," I say. "You're not from around here, are you?"

Because I'd have remembered a girl with bright red hair and crazy clothes. This isn't a town where people try to stick out. I think they just save that for when they run off to college.

She shakes her head, making her puffy red hair fly. She's got deep brown eyes the same color as mine, and she's roughly my same height and size. And that's in her clunky gunmetal-gray boots, too.

"Nope," she says, dropping her bags by the free bed. She's carrying two bags, another slung over her shoulder. "I'm about an hour away. Near Jefferson City."

"Lucky," I say. "Welcome to the middle of nowhere. Your nightly entertainment will be an old movie theater that only plays movies already on DVD and an arcade with one working pinball machine."

She laughs and hauls a suitcase—black with pink stars—onto her bed. "Sounds like a fun place to grow up."

"It's a place to grow up," I say. "But I guess I can't complain; we got the circus, after all."

"I know!" She slides the small duffel bag from her back; it's incredibly lumpy and covered in bumper stickers saying everything from DON'T TEMPT DRAGONS to SAVE THE HUMANS! "I've been waiting all school year for this."

I've known her less than five minutes, and I can already tell she's going to be a fun roommate. When she starts pulling juggling pins and netless tennis rackets from her bag, my thoughts are confirmed.

"Let me guess," I say. I flop down on my bed and watch her unpack her bag of tricks. "You're a juggler?"

"How could you tell?" she asks. "Was it the hair?"

"Totally. Jugglers always have weird hair."

"Goes with the territory. What about you? What's your focus?"

"Flying trapeze," I say. No hesitation.

"Really? Huh."

"What?"

"It's just that I didn't know they had a flying trapeze school here."

"They don't," I say slowly. And that's when it dawns on me: she's already a juggler. She's been doing this for years. Crap.

"Oh," she says. She stops rummaging through her bag and sits on her bed, facing me. There's barely three feet between us—I don't know how two college kids can live in here for a full year. "Have you done classes somewhere else?"

"Nope. It's just something I've always wanted to do."

She nods. "I don't mean to be rude, but you do know you have to try out for that department, right?"

"Yeah, I know," I say. "I saw it in the flier. But, I dunno. I've always wanted to do it. It sounds stupid, but I guess I just know it's something I'll be good at." I decide not to tell her that Leena said I looked like a natural—I'm starting to think maybe she was just being nice.

Riley shrugs. "Not stupid. I felt that way about juggling and learned a basic three-ball pass in five minutes."

"I . . . honestly, I have no idea what that means."

Her grin goes wider. Her cheeks are covered in freckles; she looks like one of those girls who's used to smiling a lot.

"I'll show you," she says. She rummages in the bag beside her and pulls out six multicolored juggling balls. "A three-ball pass is the basic juggling form," she says. Then she tosses three to me.

"Oh, I don't juggle," I say, though now that I think of it, I don't think I've actually ever tried before.

"Come on," she says. "You gotta try at least."

My first impulse is to say no, that's okay, I just want to see you try. But that's the old Jennifer. Today, right now, I'm Jennifer reinvented, and I'm not going to turn down any opportunity. I mean, how many times in my life do I have the chance to be taught juggling by a girl with fire-engine hair? I pick up the balls from where they landed on the bed and watch her.

"Okay, it goes like this. Start with two balls in one hand, one in the other. I always start with two in the right because I'm right handed, but everyone's different."

I follow her lead and put two in my right hand.

"Now, you're going to toss the one from your right hand into the air, trying make its apex just above eye level. Like this." She tosses the ball up in a perfect arc, its peak right below her hairline, and catches it without even moving her left hand. "You try."

I do. And, much to my surprise, it's a pretty good toss. The ball lands just beside my left hand.

"Nice," she says. I smile. "Okay, now with the second toss. Don't try to catch it just yet. You want to throw the ball in your left hand when the first ball is at its peak. Once you've done that, you're going to throw the third ball when the second is at its peak. Got it?"

I nod. "I think so."

She demonstrates, tossing her balls up in a steady rhythm and letting them fall on the bed. I mimic her.

"Nice," she says again. "I think you've got the hang of it. Now we try it with the catch. Remember, you don't want to have to move your hands around too much, and you definitely don't want to throw the balls forward or back or else you'll be running all over the place trying to catch them. Always throw the next ball when the other has reached the apex. Rinse and repeat."

She picks up the balls and tosses them in the air a few times, making clean catches and tosses—the balls are a blurred arc in front of her face. I lose track of how many times she tosses before she stops and looks at me.

"Your turn."

I try.

The first few catches are a disaster—I'm so focused on catching the first ball that I forget to toss the next. When I do remember, I end up throwing it at the closed window. Thankfully, the balls are just hacky sacks, so the window doesn't break. I have to give Riley credit: she doesn't laugh at all. Just watches me and gives me little pointers like "Don't move your torso so much" or "You're not trying to hit the ceiling! It's a gentle toss."

After about five minutes, she stops watching me and goes back to unpacking. I'm hooked, though, and I don't stop practicing. Not until I've managed six tosses in a row. And that takes a good ten minutes.

"Not bad," she says. She managed to unpack everything in the time it took me to get the pass down. "You're definitely starting to get the hang of it." She glances at her watch. "Just in time, too. I think we've got the intro meeting in a few minutes. Do you have any idea where the gym is?"

I nod. "Yeah, I've been there a few times. My mom used to be a secretary here, and we went to a few games."

"Funny. I wouldn't peg you for a basketball sort of girl."

"I'm not. Band nerd all the way. But I'll never say no to free popcorn and an excuse to watch a bunch of college boys running around."

Her smile is huge.

"We're going to be good friends, Jennifer," she says. She hops off the bed and takes my elbow with hers, prom style.

"Definitely."